"How much?"

"Beg your pardon?"

"How much is Mr. Slocum's bail?"

"Is that the varmint's name? I hadn't bothered to ask."

Slocum stared hard at the woman, trying to remember where they had met. Anyone this beautiful would have made an impression, and he couldn't remember ever having seen her before a few minutes ago. But that didn't make any sense. He had never met her, yet she knew his name—and she wanted to fork over bail money to get him out of jail.

"How much?" She pulled out a wad of greenbacks big enough to choke a cow. Slocum was positive now that he didn't know her. Not only was she lovely, she was rich. That combination in such a beautiful woman would have stuck in his memory to his dying day.

JAKE LOGAN

SLOCUM AND THE LADY DETECTIVE

JOVE BOOKS, NEW YORK

THE BERKLEY PUBLISHING GROUP
Published by the Penguin Group
Penguin Group (USA) Inc.
375 Hudson Street, New York, New York 10014, USA
Penguin Group (Canada), 90 Eglinton Avenue East, Suite 700, Toronto, Ontario M4P 2Y3, Canada
(a division of Pearson Penguin Canada Inc.)
Penguin Books Ltd., 80 Strand, London WC2R 0RL, England
Penguin Group Ireland, 25 St. Stephen's Green, Dublin 2, Ireland (a division of Penguin Books Ltd.)
Penguin Group (Australia), 250 Camberwell Road, Camberwell, Victoria 3124, Australia
(a division of Pearson Australia Group Pty. Ltd.)
Penguin Books India Pvt. Ltd., 11 Community Centre, Panchsheel Park, New Delhi—110 017, India
Penguin Group (NZ), 67 Apollo Drive, Rosedale, North Shore 0632, New Zealand
(a division of Pearson New Zealand Ltd.)
Penguin Books (South Africa) (Pty.) Ltd., 24 Sturdee Avenue, Rosebank, Johannesburg 2196,
South Africa

Penguin Books Ltd., Registered Offices: 80 Strand, London WC2R 0RL, England

This is a work of fiction. Names, characters, places, and incidents either are the product of the author's imagination or are used fictitiously, and any resemblance to actual persons, living or dead, business establishments, events, or locales is entirely coincidental.

SLOCUM AND THE LADY DETECTIVE

A Jove Book / published by arrangement with the author

PRINTING HISTORY
Jove edition / March 2011

Copyright © 2011 by Penguin Group (USA) Inc.
Cover illustration by Sergio Giovine.

ISBN: 978-0-515-14906-7

JOVE®
Jove Books are published by The Berkley Publishing Group,
a division of Penguin Group (USA) Inc.
375 Hudson Street, New York, New York 10014.
JOVE® is a registered trademark of Penguin Group (USA) Inc.
The "J" design is a trademark of Penguin Group (USA) Inc.

PRINTED IN THE UNITED STATES OF AMERICA

10 9 8 7 6 5 4 3 2 1

1

"Double or nothing," the scrawny kid said. He looked around furtively, as if somebody would stop him from offering to match coins.

John Slocum flipped his twenty-dollar gold piece in the air, letting it catch the brilliant sunlight that made it almost impossible not to squint. At this time of year in Leadville, Colorado, the spring sun burned the flesh even as the nip in the wind remaining from winter caused an occasional shiver. Slocum thought it was about the best feeling ever. Unless he could do the boy out of forty dollars.

"You don't look like you have it."

"You callin' me a cheat? Of course I got the money. Got forty dollars, and I'll put it up 'gainst your double eagle."

Slocum was feeling his oats. He had ridden into town from Denver through Mosquito Pass, had endured deep snow-drifts and an avalanche along the way, and yet had arrived in high spirits for no reason other than winter was finally slipping into memory.

"Get your coin," Slocum said. He watched the boy fumble out a gold piece matching his own. He still wasn't sure the boy—he looked maybe sixteen—had a second coin or why he was so willing to bet double or nothing on a single flip.

"I'll count. We both go on three. We match," the youngster said, "I owe you forty. We don't match, you owe me forty."

"Whoa, hold on," Slocum said. "That's not double or nothing. Those are even odds." He didn't want to risk what he didn't have. Twenty dollars was a princely sum, considering how terrible his luck had been at the Denver poker tables. He was lucky to have anything in his pocket and wouldn't have if he hadn't found one last speck of good luck that won him a small pot at the Thieves Den Gambling Emporium just off Larimer Square. His winnings secured in his vest pocket next to his brother's watch, he had left the game, left the gaming parlor, mounted his mare, and ridden due west hunting for a pass through the Front Range. Luck was a fickle bitch, and Denver had exhausted his chances for another winning hand.

Leadville had to be better, and if this punk kid was any example, it would be.

"All right, even odds. You still want to match?" The youngster nervously ran his fingers around the rim of his coin.

"No."

"What? You can't . . ." The kid glared at him. "Oh, all right. I'm feelin' mighty lucky today. Double or nothing."

"If I win, you pay forty," Slocum said, to be sure. It amused him the way his would-be gambling partner looked as if he had bitten into a sour persimmon.

"Yeah, yeah. Let's do it. One, two, three."

Slocum flipped his coin on the count of three and seldom had he seen a hand so fast. Dirty fingers shot out and snared his double eagle in midair. The boy turned and started to run, only to slip on a patch of ice and fall facedown in the mud. Two quick steps put Slocum next to the young man. Before the cheater could get his feet under him, Slocum shoved him down into the cold, sticky mud with the sole of his boot.

"That wasn't very neighborly," he said. The youngster sputtered. Slocum let him get to his hands and knees but kept him in the mud to teach him a lesson. "You have the money? Or were you lying?"

"I ain't no liar!"

Slocum said nothing. An angry, mud-caked face turned up to him. Sullenly, the young man fumbled in his pocket and drew out two coins, both as filthy as their owner. Their former owner.

Slocum took them and tucked the golden coins into his vest pocket. When the young man tried to stand, Slocum shoved him back.

"Now, give me back my coin. The one you snatched."

With a quirky smile, the teenager pulled a coin from his pocket and handed it up to Slocum.

"Cain't fault a man for tryin', now can you?"

"I can. If you were a couple years older, I would have shot you as you ran."

"If I was a couple years older, I'd be wearin' a hogleg on my hip and you wouldna dared!"

Slocum had to admit the boy was quick. His hand had flashed out to grab the coin very neatly. Put a six-gun in a holster and let the boy draw and it would be a deadly combination. Slocum knew, though, that it took more than quick reflexes to be a gunfighter. He wasn't sure the boy had the killer instinct required to pull the trigger.

Looking down at the muddy, pathetic figure, he doubted it.

"Get yourself an honest job. Stealing from strangers will get you killed."

"Go to hell."

Amid a flurry of flying mud, the boy slipped and slid and finally found enough purchase to run off. Slocum watched him go, shaking his head. Leadville was a mining town and a prosperous one to boot, surrounded by proven silver mines.

If the youngster had tried this trick with a drunk miner, he might have gotten away with the theft—he probably had many times over if he had forty dollars to wager. Slocum considered finding others the boy had robbed, then decided against it. With sixty dollars riding high in his pocket, he could dare Lady Luck once more and have a chance of walking away with even more. Miners were notoriously bad card players, and for whatever reason, the less successful they were at finding blue dirt, the worse they were at poker.

Some men couldn't catch a break if it was hog-tied and thrown onto their doorstep.

Slocum avoided the deeper mud holes in Leadville's main street as he made his way to a restaurant that didn't look as likely to poison him as the one serving up slop in a tent a few yards down the street. The smell from that place caused his belly to rumble—and not in a good way.

He stepped into the restaurant and saw red-and-white-checked tablecloths and silverware set out for the patrons.

"Set yourself down anywhere," the rail-thin waiter said. "You want the special or you want somethin' special?"

"What's the difference?"

"Not much," the waiter said, scratching himself. "One's steak and eggs and the other's eggs and steak."

"I'll have that, eggs runny and steak rare."

"It'll moo when you stab it with the fork," the waiter promised.

And Slocum couldn't find any flaw in the meal. It came exactly as he had ordered and slid down into his gullet, chased all the way with hot coffee. When he'd finished, he leaned back and felt as content as any time he could remember.

"That'll be two-fifty, mister," the waiter said.

"Mighty steep prices, but it was a mighty good steak," Slocum said, fishing out one of his three double eagles and passing it over.

The waiter took it, then frowned. He bit down hard on it,

then grabbed the knife off the plate holding the remains of Slocum's meal. The man dug the knife point into the coin, then tossed it onto the table.

It spun and dropped with a dull thud.

"Gimme real money. That there's a lead slug that's been painted gold."

Slocum pulled another coin from his pocket and dug his fingernail into it. The gilding came off and left his dirty fingernail shiny.

"That's all right," Slocum said. "I've got a real gold coin here." He pulled out his original coin, then stopped and stared at it as it lay in the palm of his hand.

Part of the milling around the edge had broken free, showing dull gray metal beneath.

"Son of a bitch," he said, slamming the coin down hard on the table next to the other two.

"That kid swindled me!"

Slocum ran back his memory of what had happened. When the youngster had snatched the coin, he had stuck it away in his pocket. Slocum's demand to be paid had allowed the muddy thief to press three fake coins on him, keeping the real gold double eagle hidden away. For the price of three lead slugs and getting dirty, which he hardly noticed, the youngster had swindled Slocum out of twenty dollars.

His only twenty dollars. He didn't even have a nickel left.

"I don't much care for your sob story, mister," the waiter said. "I want my money."

"I was robbed," Slocum said, "but I'll find him and get it back." He started to rise, but the scrawny man clamped down on his shoulder with surprising strength and forced him into the chair.

"I ain't lettin' you out of my sight till you work off the meal. You want, I call the marshal. He's one mean son of a buck and as likely to beat you to death as drag you to his godforsaken jail. The only good thing 'bout that jail's that I feed the prisoners. The bad thing is that the marshal makes you pay for it. What do you want to do, mister?"

Slocum's mind raced. The man was no match for him if it came down to a fight, but Slocum didn't have a quarrel with him. Eating a meal and then trying to pay for it with worthless slugs had to look as if a cheat had come into the restaurant.

Slocum was no cheat.

"I'll work it off." He stood, took the plates, and started for the kitchen. "You got hot water ready to wash the plates?"

"Out back. Build a fire and get it started." Slocum was halfway there went the waiter called, "You ain't gonna run, are you?"

The look Slocum gave him forced the man to clamp his mouth shut. The answer was written on Slocum's face. He was an honest man and would give an honest day's work to pay for what he'd eaten.

And he did.

It was well past sundown when Slocum finished the last of the chores and went inside. He had chopped a pile of wood for the cooking stove, had built a stack of clean plates and utensils, and had done what he could to keep the restaurant floor swept clean during the day. With the constant traffic of hungry miners and drifters coming through, knocking mud off their boots as they walked, it had been like moving all the dirt in one big hole to another and then back. He ended up where he started and there wasn't anything to show for the entire day's work. Nothing except satisfaction in paying off his debt.

"What more do you need?" Slocum asked.

The waiter, who also cooked and, Slocum supposed, owned the restaurant, shrugged. He glanced over his shoulder at a rough customer sitting near the door.

"I'll give you dinner if you'll watch that one. From the

way you carry that six-shooter of yours, you're no stranger to fightin'."

"Done my share," Slocum allowed. And he had, ever since the war. He wasn't proud of having ridden with Quantrill and he sure as hell wasn't proud of the way he'd killed the carpetbagger judge who had tried to steal his family farm back in Calhoun, Georgia. Slocum didn't think that was a mistake but judge killing, even when they needed it, was a crime that would dog his heels until some unknown undertaker tossed dirt in his cold, dead face.

But Slocum wasn't the sort to allow a phony claim of unpaid taxes to carry the day. The judge and his hired gunman had met their fate, Slocum had buried the both of them, then he had ridden west and never slowed down to see what tracked him.

"Men like that sit by the door, thinkin' on eatin', then dartin' outside without payin'."

"You want me to collect from him?"

"Naw, I'll do that. Just be ready to tackle him if he tries to run."

The waiter hitched up the apron that kept sliding down his snake hips, then went to the table and stood over the man. He cleared his throat and said, "You owe four dollars fer the meal and dessert. You want to pay up now?"

"You're a pushy whoreson, ain't you?" The man—a cowboy, if Slocum could tell, and on the run from the law—dug his heels into the floorboard and pushed himself back, legs straight so his hand would have a clear path to his six-shooter at his right hip.

"Don't want trouble, just want my money. You et, you pay."

"Here, and be damned." The cowboy tossed a coin on the table, stood, and shoved the waiter back. In three strides he was out the door and swallowed up by the night.

"That's a relief," the waiter said, picking up the coin. He frowned, bit into it, then flung it away so hard it sounded like a bullet ricocheting off the wall. "Fake. The bastard gave me a fake double eagle."

Slocum picked up the coin and examined it. For all he could tell, it was the twin of those he had been given earlier. What might have been an isolated occurrence was taking on the air of a flood of bad coins.

He ran his finger over the yellowed surface and pushed away a veneer of gold. Nothing felt like gold. And beneath the surface lay gray metal better suited to making a bullet than a coin.

Slocum went outside and looked around the main street. Already miners were pouring in from their dreary work underground, pushing and shoving to get into the saloons and the Tabor Opera House down the street, where some chanteuse claiming to be from France was ready to warble all night long for the hefty price of admission.

"You see 'im? Where'd the thievin', sneaky son of a bitch go?" The waiter pushed Slocum aside and waved around a meat cleaver. "I'll cut off his hands so he'll never pass no bogus money in this town again. Leastways, not to me!"

"There's something of an epidemic of fake coins," Slocum said. He could search all night and not find the cowboy, but he stopped and looked hard across the street into the shadows of an alley. "What's it worth if I get your money?"

"Free meals for a week, and I'll be much obliged, Mr.—"

"Slocum."

"I need you to make an example of him, Mr. Slocum. I don't want any of them damn fool miners thinkin' they can do the same as he done to me. It'd be worth it if they showed me some respect. I—"

Slocum left the man grumbling on the doorstep of his restaurant and crossed to the alley. He pressed his back against the wall and listened hard. A smile crept to his lips when he heard, "Double or nothin', mister."

"For a twenty-dollar gold piece? You don't have that kind of money, kid."

"I do!"

Slocum had found the youngster who had stolen his double eagle earlier. He started to enter the alleyway and confront the sneak thief, then pressed back into the wall and thought on it. Wherever the young man got the coins was the place Slocum wanted. He had a suspicion he would find not only his own coin there but the cowboy from the restaurant and maybe a lot of others intent on switching real coins for their fake ones.

"Damn, you won," came an aggrieved complaint. "That ain't a two-headed coin now, is it, boy?"

"I won fair and square. See?"

Slocum imagined the young man holding up his coin as he took the real one and tucked it away. In the dark, it was good enough to pass for real—and it undoubtedly had both a head and a tail. He had been lucky and won this time and didn't need to waste one of the counterfeit coins on a switch, as he had with Slocum.

"I'd go you again but all I got's some scrip," the victim said.

"Don't like paper money. Only specie. Gold coins. Maybe silver. But metal, not paper. Why, anybody could print up a bale of that there paper money and make us think it was worth something."

Before his victim could reply, the young thief came bustling out of the alley, arms swinging, chest puffed up, and his head high. He had made another easy twenty dollars. Working in the mine for a month would hardly bring him that much money, and he had snookered the man in the wink of an eye.

Slocum wondered if he would continue working the street until he'd foisted off all the imitation coins or if he had to return with the gold coins he stole after every sucker. The answer came fast. The young man stopped in the street and waved. Slocum stepped under a broad awning when he saw the man in the second-story window of the hotel. He had found the cowboy from the restaurant and had confirmed to his own satisfaction that a counterfeiting ring was working to fleece the people of Leadville.

The youngster dashed for the hotel and went inside. Slocum followed more slowly, going through the front door and looking around the hotel parlor to be sure the two crooks weren't conducting their business in plain sight.

"You lookin' fer a room, mister? Got one left. Real busy tonight."

"My kid got away from me. I thought he ducked in here. You see him?" Slocum described the scrawny young confidence man.

"Uh, I dunno." The clerk obviously had seen the boy but wasn't looking for trouble in his hotel.

"He was hunting for his uncle—my brother. He was supposed to get to town today, but I haven't seen him either."

"What's he look like?" The clerk's suspicions soared, then abated when Slocum described the cowboy from the restaurant the best he could.

"Yeah, he's got a room. Second floor, up front. Looks out over the street, just like he asked. Reckon he wanted to watch for you."

"He's like that, my brother."

"Don't look a thing like you," the clerk said, again suspicious.

"Different papas. What was the room number?"

Before the clerk could reply, the youngster came back down the stairs, stopped, spotted Slocum, and let out a loud cry of warning.

Slocum raced to the stairs and took them three at a time. The altitude took the energy out of him and left him struggling to breathe. He bent forward, hands on his knees, to take a moment to recover when the door burst open and the cowboy came out, his six-shooter drawn.

"You ain't gettin' a dime outta me."

From the back of the hall came the loud cry, "He's the one I snookered earlier. He knows!" The loud slam of a door told Slocum one of his quarry had hightailed it down the back stairs and into the night. That left him with only the cowboy in the doorway.

"I want my money back," Slocum said. "All of it."

He tossed his head to one side so the stiff brim of his hat snapped against the wall, sending the Stetson spinning to the floor. The instant of distraction was all Slocum could buy with the tactic. He slapped leather and dragged out his Colt Navy from his cross-draw holster.

Both his Colt and the cowboy's black powder Remington discharged at the same instant. The difference came in accuracy. A huge chuck of plaster exploded from the wall to Slocum's right. His bullet caught the cowboy in the gut and doubled him over. Another shot from the Remington went into the floorboards. As the cowboy fought to straighten and get off a better-aimed shot, Slocum ended the conflict with a bullet to the man's forehead.

The cowboy sagged to his knees, then fell face forward onto the floor. His blood oozed out and stained the threadbare carpet.

Slocum stepped forward, wary although he knew his second shot had been fatal.

"Drop that gun or, I swear, I'll cut you in half. I got this here shotgun barrel crammed with carpet tacks and I don't miss—ever."

Slocum looked back over his shoulder down the stairs where a man wearing a marshal's badge held a ponderous 10-gauge shotgun in rock-steady hands.

He dropped his Colt and raised his hands. Explaining was better than dying.

2

"This yahoo was trying to rob me," Slocum said, his fingers twitching as he kept them above his head.

"That remains to be seen." The marshal shoved him away, down the hall, to better examine the body on the floor. "You shot him twice."

"He fired at me twice." Slocum started to point to the hole in the plaster wall but the marshal poked at him with the shotgun. The lawman hadn't been fibbing about the tacks in the barrel. A room cleaner like this would hardly leave a bloody smear on the walls as testament to where John Slocum had once stood. With a weapon like this, the marshal could keep control over a bar full of drunken miners—and he'd probably used it more than once from the look of the pitted, scratched bore.

"That's not much of a story. This gent waltzes on out of his room as you come by, sticks a gun in your face to rob you, the pair of you shoot it out, and then he's drawing flies on the floor?"

Slocum nodded.

"Clerk tells a different story."

"They always do."

"He called for me when he saw your interest in this gent and a kid."

"You search his room and you'll find a bag filled with fake coins."

"You need to find a story and stick with it. Getting all wild and woolly about your accusations doesn't do a damned thing to make me believe you. Fact is, the crazier the story you spin, the more likely I am to think you knocked on his door and just gunned him down."

"How do you explain that his gun's been fired? And the hole in the hallway wall?"

"I can tell you just blowed into town," the marshal said, standing and stepping across the body into the sleeping room. "How do I know? Shoot-outs happen in this hotel, sometimes two or three a night when it's payday at the mines. Other times, it's real quiet. Won't be a killing here for two-three days." He looked around the room to be sure it was empty, then motioned with the shotgun for Slocum to precede him down the stairs.

All the way down to the lobby Slocum felt an itch along his spine, waiting for the marshal to stumble on the steep staircase and discharge both barrels into him. That was ridiculous, and he knew it. If the lawman shot just one barrel, Slocum would never know it. He'd be a goner before his body could tumble the rest of the way down the stairs.

"Got a body upstairs, Jethro," the marshal called. Slocum watched the lawman's face reflected in a dirty mirror hanging near the door and saw that he never took his attention off his prisoner. "Get the undertaker to drag it over to the parlor. And don't you go stealing anything from his saddlebags either. I already rummaged through them a mite and know what's in there."

"I'd never do a thing like that, Marshal Atkinson. You know me."

"That's why I'm telling you not to steal anything, Jethro."

"He'll end up with a bag of fake coins," Slocum said.

"Now there, I don't need advice from the likes of you. Turn left and walk down the middle of the street. If I have to shoot you, I don't want blood spattering all over the board-walk and walls. The businessmen of this here town get up-set when they have to scrub off blood, especially when it's from some stranger who don't matter one whit."

"I'd think they wouldn't mind so much as long as it wasn't their own blood."

This produced a chuckle from the marshal.

Slocum half turned and saw movement in the shadows. The scrawny kid who had fled just before the shooting started faded back into darkness. Slocum thought he heard foot-falls on the hotel's back staircase but couldn't be sure. If the youngster returned to the room, he'd steal any money there—and any of the counterfeit coins. Something about the way he moved brought a caution from the lawman.

"You're thinking. Don't go doing that. I haven't killed anybody all day and want to make it to midnight 'fore I do."

Slocum glumly walked to the town lockup, a rundown building with a steeply sloped roof to let the heavy winter snowfall slide off easily. He went inside and almost backed out. Only Marshal Atkinson's shotgun in his back kept him from retreating.

"Why do you keep it so hot in here?" Slocum asked.

"Winters are brutal and these old bones prefer warm. I'd be in Mexico sitting in some cantina drinking gut-burning tequila with a pretty señorita on my knee if I had enough money." He prodded Slocum forward. "That cell. The first one. It's yours till I figure out what's going on."

The heavy iron bar door clanked shut behind Slocum. He turned and examined the jail for the first time. Sweat beaded his forehead, and all of wasn't caused by the stove glowing red-hot in the center of the room. The exterior of the jail might be dilapidated, but Atkinson maintained the interior—and the cells—with an eye toward perfection.

Slocum hunted for a speck of rust. The bars were clean of any spot where he might attack the failing metal with any hope of escaping. The cell was more of a cage with thick iron straps going above and on two sides. He guessed they might run under the dirt floor. The wall with the door in it was secure, and Atkinson had placed his desk far enough away that, even if Slocum grew arms ten feet long, he wasn't going to snare the keys off the top or from the peg on the wall behind the desk chair. A rack of rifles along the exterior wall was even more distant. A chain ran through the trigger guards and fastened them with a heavy padlock.

"I got the key right here," Atkinson said, fishing for a string around his neck. He held out a key that would fit the padlock. "I been at this job for nigh on eight years, and I've seen every kind of escape attempt. Men have tried to tunnel out. Can't do it. Chew through the bars—one gent broke his store-bought teeth trying that. Some had friends who tried to shoot their way in. They didn't make it, 'cept out to the graveyard. Another tried to use dynamite to blow open the back wall. All he did was blow himself to kingdom come. No, sir, the only way out of that cell is for me to let you out."

"You might as well let me out now, then," Slocum said, "since I haven't done anything."

The marshal pulled Slocum's six-shooter from his belt and held it up to a coal oil lamp to get a better look.

"I've seen shootists come and go. Most don't have a pistol this finely balanced. The ebony handle's worn from use. The whole weapon is well used and even better taken care of. Why, I've seen cowboys with lumps of rust in their holsters. But this is a precision six-shooter, and unless I miss my guess, you're mighty quick with it."

Slocum said nothing.

"It might just turn out to be the way you said, how that gent ended up dead in the hotel corridor. Might be just a spat between the two of you went bad. Or it could be somebody hired himself a professional gunman to kill a rival."

Slocum sat on the edge of the bunk. The mattress was thin but not as thin as the blanket. With the way the marshal kept that stove stoked, though, no prisoner would ever need a blanket.

"Don't even think on it. It's been tried and it doesn't work."

"What?" Slocum looked up, startled.

"Toss the mattress or blanket over the stove and start 'em smoking so I'll open the cell door to let you out before the whole damned place burns down. It won't happen. I'll let you choke on the smoke and die inside."

"I'll keep that in mind."

"Do. As I said, the only way out of here is if I let you leave."

Slocum lay back on the bunk, the garrulous old marshal rattling on about the desperados he'd locked up and how many of them had been sent to prison. Staring overhead didn't inspire much confidence in his ability to get out of the cell. The inch-wide iron straps were securely riveted into a wicker basket pattern that made any attempt on his part to pry one band free utterly futile.

"I'll get one of my deputies to bring back the dead gent's belongings so I can go through them. Right now, all my deputies are occupied in the saloons. Won't be long before you have a companion or two for the night. Miners can't hold their liquor, not that I've ever noticed."

Slocum considered trying to escape so the marshal would shoot him and put him out of his misery. The heat from the stove was so much that Slocum's shirt was plastered to his body with sweat. But worst of all was the incessant flood of reminisces and cautions about trying to escape.

"I hear somebody coming now. Reckon that might be Lem or maybe Sid, my top deputies. I'll—"

The marshal stopped his verbal diarrhea and stood. Slocum swung his boots off the bunk and sat up at the vision of loveliness who seemed to float into the jailhouse. She stood about five-foot-five and had a trim waist held in by an expensive dress. Slocum was no expert, but he thought it must have come from back East, with silk ribbons and frilly doodads on it. She stopped just inside the doorway, patted back a strand of auburn hair, then pointedly ignored Slocum as she went to stand in front of the marshal's desk.

"Evening, ma'am. You got the right place? This is the town jail."

"You must be Marshal Atkinson," she said, thrusting out a hand clad in a glove trimmed with delicate lace. "I am Miss Elena Warburton of the Chicago Warburtons."

"Don't rightly know what that means, but I'm pleased to make your acquaintance. I'd offer a chair, but the only one I had got busted up last week and I haven't had time to replace it."

"That is quite all right. I shan't be long. I am here to bail out that gentleman."

Marshal Atkinson made a show of looking around, then smirked.

"Don't see a gentleman anywhere, leastways not that a fine lady like you would appreciate."

"How much?"

"Beg your pardon?"

"How much is Mr. Slocum's bail?"

"Is that the varmint's name? I hadn't bothered to ask."

Slocum stared hard at the woman, trying to remember where they had met. Anyone this beautiful would have made an impression, and he couldn't remember ever having seen her before a few minutes ago. But that didn't make any sense. He had never met her, yet she knew his name—and she wanted to fork over bail money to get him out of jail.

"How much?" She pulled out a wad of greenbacks big enough to choke a cow. Slocum was positive now that he didn't know her. Not only was she lovely, she was rich. That combination in such a beautiful woman would have stuck in his memory to his dying day.

"Whoa, little lady," Atkinson said. "Put that roll of bills away." He rubbed his stubbled chin as he looked hard at her. Elena's brown eyes never wavered under his hard examination. "I haven't set bail since I don't know what he's done."

"It was not murder," she said.

Slocum was even more intrigued by her. She was a stranger, yet she knew his name and what had happened back at the hotel, at least as far as a man being killed.

"How'd you know a thing like that?"

"I saw the entire sordid affair. The other man came from his room, gun drawn. Mr. Slocum was the victim of a failed robbery attempt. Gunshots were exchanged and the robber swallowed a pill he could not digest."

"Slocum's lead pill," Atkinson said, still rubbing his chin. "How'd you come to see it all?"

"I had just opened my door to leave my room for a late meal when I saw it all. I wasn't ten feet away."

Slocum knew she was lying. He would have seen her because he had watched the dead man's scrawny accomplice hightail it down that hall to the back stairs. But he didn't much care that she claimed to see what she hadn't because the marshal was buying it.

"Do tell. That changes everything, doesn't it? You're one lucky gent, Slocum, having a fine lady like this stand up for you."

Slocum noticed that the marshal made no move for the key ring dangling on the peg. Something had made the wily lawman suspicious.

"Tell me, Miss Warburton, why would a perfect stranger like you want to put up bail money for a man like Slocum? You said you didn't know him."

"I told you, sir. I am Elena Warburton of the Chicago Warburtons."

"So?" This puzzled the marshal. He wasn't alone. Slocum wondered how that explained anything.

"We have devoted a great deal of money and effort to preventing the innocent from suffering. We fund charities for the poor, and my father is an attorney who does a considerable amount of *pro bono* work. That means he defends men for free."

"Reckon I've heard the term, though not much of that's done in a town like Leadville. Either a defendant hires himself a lawyer or does the job on his own. Hard enough to get a lawyer in these parts who's not entirely interested in feathering his own nest with mining claims and suing over claim jumping."

"Then you will release him? He is, on my word, innocent of the crime of murder."

"He did shoot down that gent, though?"

"He did. It was self-defense."

"No call to throw anyone in the jug for protecting himself, though Jethro—he's the room clerk at the hotel—did say Slocum here was acting mighty nervy."

"I don't know about that. I saw what I saw and—"

"And you're Miss Elena Warburton of the Chicago Warburtons," the marshal finished.

"Do not mock me, sir."

"Sorry," Atkinson said, but Slocum heard no apology in the word. "It's just that we don't get much in the way of, well, Warburtons out here."

Elena Warburton stood her ground, gaze icy and fixed on the marshal. Slocum saw the slow change come to Atkinson and then the marshal reached over, grabbed the keys, and released Slocum.

"Don't go leaving town till I say so, Mr. Slocum," the lawman said. "When the undertaker's looked over the body and verified what Miss Warburton says, you can go to hell in your own way. But not till I say so."

"Much obliged," Slocum said, looking at the lovely woman.

"Just doing my duty," Atkinson said as if Slocum had addressed him. He handed over Slocum's gun belt and six-shooter. Slocum had it strapped around his waist before he left the jail.

Stepping out into the night was like a fist punching him. He turned to ice all over as the cold spring night closed in on his sweat-drenched body.

"I am glad to get away from that furnace," Elena said.

"Why?"

"Because it is uncomfortable," the woman said.

"Why'd you lie to get me out? You didn't see anything."

"How can you know that?" She turned to him. Her brown eyes carried glints of gold. A hint of a smile graced her bow-shaped lips.

"I don't miss much, especially when my life's on the line. I would have seen you, even if you were just peeking out an open door. But you would have had to step into the hall to see since the doors swing the wrong way for you to have seen me at the head of the stairs."

"You are more remarkable than I thought," she said.

"How do you know my name?"

"I asked Mr. Grimaldi." When she saw he had no idea who this was, she explained, "He hired you to wash his dishes and cut his cooking stove's wood."

"Never asked the restaurant owner his name."

"But he knew yours, therefore I learned it." Elena sounded smug.

"That's how you got my name but it doesn't explain anything else."

"No, it doesn't." She pointed toward the hotel. "Let's return to the scene of the crime. I am interested in the dead man's luggage, even if the marshal is not."

"The fake coins," Slocum said. "You're following a trail of counterfeit coins." He was moderately pleased to see her jump as if she had been pinched on the butt.

"You're more than observant, Mr. Slocum."

"John," he corrected her.

She nodded. "You put facts together well, John."

"Like a detective." Again he was pleased to see her reaction.

"Yes, it is so. I am a detective, and I am hunting for the source of the counterfeit coins. Mr. Grimaldi told me of your earlier contretemps with payment for a meal. It came out that you went after the second diner for paying with a newly minted bogus double eagle. That told me you knew something more of the source. Do you?"

They stopped outside the hotel. The lobby doors stood open, and Slocum saw Jethro inside, arguing with a patron.

"Let's use the back stairs," he suggested. "The room's going to be rented out, and if you want to look at the dead man's gear, we're going to have to hurry."

"You didn't answer," she said. "I have been entrusted to find the criminal making the illegal coins and arrest him. Or them."

"I don't know as much about this as you do," Slocum said, holding the door open for her. Elena paused, then brushed past him, the whiff of her perfume causing his nostrils to flare. But the way she pressed against him as she entered the upstairs hallway set his pulse pounding. He followed and then reached out and grabbed her by the shoulder.

"What?" She half turned and then he spun her around and pulled her into his arms to give her a big kiss. For a moment she tensed, then melted against him and returned the kiss.

Slocum released her as suddenly as he had grabbed her. She looked flustered but not angry at the kiss.

"The kid was picking the lock," Slocum whispered. "I didn't want him to spot me."

"What kid?"

"The owlhoot who passed the fake coins off onto me. He just broke into the hotel room his partner was using."

"His partner? You know Eakin's partner? I haven't been able—"

Slocum whirled her about and drew his six-shooter as he walked on cat's feet to the now-closed door.

From inside he heard the sound of the youngster rummaging about, hunting for either his partner's stash of bogus coins or more likely the real ones.

"What are you going to do, John?"

Slocum turned the glass doorknob slowly and tried to open the door a crack. The squeaky hinges warned the boy. Slocum slammed the door wide open and lifted his six-shooter.

Both of them shot at the same time. The youngster got off both barrels from a derringer, but all Slocum needed was one round from his Colt. The boy staggered back, then smashed the window and tumbled out into the street.

"You shot him!"

Slocum ignored Elena and ran to the broken window. There was a commotion in the street, but it wasn't because of a dead body falling from the second story of the hotel. It was because of the wounded man struggling down the crowded street.

"Go after him, John. Don't let him get away! I need to know everything he knows!"

Slocum looked into Elena's eyes and saw a glint he normally saw in a sexually aroused woman. The gunfight had excited her, even as it almost left a man dead.

3

Slocum holstered his six-gun and looked out the window. It would be a hard drop, but he heard a clamor coming from downstairs. The room clerk had finally decided he had to investigate the shots—or maybe he wouldn't rent out the room to a prospective customer without a little cleaning up.

Slocum crossed the room in three strides and slammed the door. He grabbed a chair and shoved it under the doorknob, then said to Elena, "Search the place for whatever you need."

"What're you going to do, John? That man—"

Elena spoke to thin air. Slocum returned to the window and used the pillow from the bed to sweep away glass shards. He wiggled through the small window, braced on the windowsill for a moment, and then dropped to the street, landing with a grunt. He kept from rolling to absorb the shock since that would have sent him through the now-freezing mud puddles. People stared; if he had been coated head to foot in mud, they would have stared even more.

There were only two directions the young man might have gone. Slocum headed toward the opera house, where

23

the late-night crowd was just now stumbling into the street, laughing and joking at what they had seen inside. Slocum avoided the crush, got to the boardwalk, then jumped onto a rain barrel at the side of the opera house.

He spotted his quarry instantly. A shock wave of people formed behind the stumbling boy, making it look like a boat rowing through water and leaving behind a trail. Nevertheless, like the waves in a lake, these would quickly disappear and leave no track for Slocum to follow. He swung up, caught at a drain pipe, and pulled himself up to the roof of a two-story building. He dashed across the sloping, slippery expanse, vaulted to the next building, and kept going until he found himself confronted with a three-story bank building. Only then did he drop back to the street.

The crowd was thinner here, and the stumbling boy was easier to see. He clutched his belly as he made his way toward the southern side of town. Slocum found that he could keep a safe distance between the two of them by walking slowly but steadily. The youngster lurched along, sometimes putting on a burst of speed as his strength waxed and then he almost stopped when the pain doubled him over. Slocum almost went to him.

Almost. The youth might be only sixteen or seventeen, but Slocum had faced soldiers during the war who were younger. And this sneak thief had not only stolen twenty dollars from him, he had tried to put two bullets in him.

"Nuggets," the young man gasped out, leaning against a door to a small house. For a moment Slocum thought the boy was hallucinating from the pain of carrying a bullet in his belly. He rapped again and yelled the word louder. The door opened. He had given a password.

"What happened to you?"

"Shot. Shot trying to get Ernie's coins back. Help me. God, my gut is on fire. Help me."

Slocum stepped back into shadow when the man supporting the wounded thief stepped out so he could get a

better look around. The man had his hand on a six-gun holstered at his side. Slocum held his breath when the man
looked straight at him, but the dark night saved him. The
man spun, half lifted the scrawny boy off his feet, and flung
him into the house. The door slammed behind them.

Slocum waited a few seconds, then crossed the street and
circled the house, looking for a window. All the rooms save
for the kitchen at the rear were dark. He chanced a quick
glance through a small window and saw the man he'd shot
sprawled on the table. His rescuer stood over him, glaring.

"You stupid bastard. Your brother gets killed and now you
go and take a bullet. You're just like him. You got a death
wish, too."

"Please, wasn't like that. Ernie was taken by surprise.
No idea who that gun slick is. Fast. Damned fast. Got me
and I had my pistol aimed at him. Drew and shot me 'fore I
could even pull the trigger."

The boy's recollection was shaky. Slocum had entered
the room with his Colt drawn. He could excuse the mistake
since he had taken the thief by surprise.

"Where are the slugs?"

"D-Don't know. Looked but they wasn't in Ernie's gear."

"You liar!" The man grabbed the bloody shirt front and
began shaking so hard that Slocum heard the boy's teeth
clacking together. "Tell me. I got too much ridin' on this to
be done out of it by a pair of two-bit swindlers."

"Hurt so bad. Please, get me a doc."

"The coins first. Then the doctor."

"Don't know. Ernie . . ." The boy's voice trailed off.

Slocum put his hand on his six-shooter and slowly drew
it. The time was right to snap the next link in the chain. For
all he knew, this was the crook responsible for making the
counterfeit coins and sending the likes of Ernie Eakin and
his brother out to exchange them for the real McCoy.

Slocum went to the back door and tried it. The slight
rattle warned the man inside he had a visitor. Six slugs

ripped through the flimsy wood door, sending splinters flying like tiny bullets.

Slocum flinched away, then kicked hard and knocked the door inward. He was ready to shoot, but the man was gone.

As he crossed the tiny kitchen, a feeble hand clutched at his sleeve.

"Mister, help me. Been shot. Need a doctor."

Slocum looked down. The youngster's eyes were open, but he wasn't seeing anything. The pain blurred everything so much he didn't know he appealed to the man who had put that bullet in his gut.

"Where are the slugs?" he asked, repeating what the other gang member had said.

"Don't know."

"Who was that?"

Slocum spoke to a dead man. Unseeing eyes stared up at him, and the hand gripping his sleeve slipped off, leaving bloody fingerprints.

A thousand things tumbled through Slocum's head as he considered what he ought to do. The smartest thing would be to mount up and ride on out before Marshal Atkinson got wind of yet another dead man with Slocum's bullet in him. If this kept up, Slocum would wipe out the entire Eakin family. For all he knew, he already had by shooting both Ernie and his brother, now flopped out on this table.

Too much swirled around him that he didn't know—couldn't know. Where did Elena Warburton fit into all this? She'd been hired by somebody to find the source of the counterfeit coins, but Slocum didn't think she worked for the government. If she did, she would have shown a badge to the marshal rather than lying to him. Slocum smiled ruefully at the notion of the federal government back in Washington, D.C., ever hiring a woman to investigate such a crime. Elena had to work for someone else.

Too many questions and not enough in it for Slocum. But

he began riffling through the dead man's pockets to see what he could find. A single twenty-dollar gold piece tumbled into his palm when he tore off a vest pocket. Slocum held it up and tried to decide if it was real. He ran his finger across the milled edge and the ridges didn't flake off.

So far, so good. He bit down on the coin and looked at his dental imprint, then stuck the coin into his pocket. He had his twenty dollars back. This was a real coin.

But he had been duped, he had been used, and he didn't like any of that. For whatever reason, Elena had gotten him out of jail, and he owed her for that. How much he wasn't sure, but he owed her. He was a man who always paid his debts.

Slocum finished searching the corpse and found a scrap of paper, mostly destroyed from being soaked in water and caked with mud. He carefully spread the sheet out against the wall and let the water drip out. Plastered at eye level, the smeary ink lines revealed a map. Slocum turned his head a little to get a better orientation, located Leadville and the road going northward, along the railroad tracks, and then a dotted line diverging and going into a valley. There might have been an X at this spot, but the paper had been torn away so he could only guess at that.

Tracking the owlhoot who had waited in this house for the Eakin boy would be impossible in the dark. Given the size of the town, melting into the crowd of drunken miners would be easy enough. Or he could have ridden away, out of town, away from Colorado, to leave behind what he had to see as a bloodbath that just might include him if he stayed around much longer. Two of his partners had been cut down in the span of a few hours. Any sensible man would take that as a warning.

Still, Slocum doubted the unknown man had left. He, like the Eakin brothers, was likely part of a bigger gang. Making the fake coins was beyond the skill of either of the men Slocum had shot. They were confidence men whose job would have been to convert the bogus coins to real ones, either through gambling swindles or purchasing goods and using them or reselling them at a discount to others looking for a bargain and who had legitimate money.

A last look at the map etched the details into Slocum's mind. Somewhere along the way he had come to a conclusion. It was probably a dangerous one, but he was curious and wanted answers. He opened the back door and stepped out, then froze. Carried on the cold night air came the sound of approaching horses.

"I tell you, Marshal, there's a dead man in the old Fulton house."

"Shut up, Lem," came the voice Slocum had never wanted to hear again. Atkinson and a companion, likely a deputy, had almost caught him.

Slocum slipped back inside, glanced at the boy's body, and then went to the front of the house. The door here opened out onto a trail winding away into the dark. Rather than leaving immediately, he chanced a quick look outside and saw two men moving closer. The darkness hid their identity, but they had to be deputies. Atkinson intended to close in from front and back, trapping him inside.

Did Atkinson know the identity of his quarry? Or was he just playing it safe since his deputy had spotted a body inside? Slocum frowned. How had Lem seen anything inside the house and had time to go fetch the marshal?

"Now!" The shout from the rear warned Slocum the lawmen were coming in from both sides simultaneously. He swung around behind the front door as it slammed open. The two deputies raced inside, waving their guns around.

"Back. They're in the back!" The deputies crossed the small room and burst into the kitchen as Atkinson and Lem came in.

Slocum helped matters along a mite by drawing his sixshooter and firing into the ceiling.

Each of the lawmen thought the other had fired. Lead

flew like deadly bees throughout the small house, giving Slocum the chance to slip around the door and duck outside. Long strides took him along the rocky trail leading up the hill. Behind him he heard Marshal Atkinson screeching for his men to stop firing.

A stream of curses followed the order, and finally the echoing gunfire died down as Atkinson regained control of his men. The ambush had been clever, but the deputies had been too keyed up and ready to shoot at anything moving for it to be effective.

Slocum reached the top of the ridge. He sat on a rock to catch his breath. From the angle where he sat, he saw deep hoofprints in the soft ground. Bending over, he ran his finger around the edge and saw it was still sharp, half-frozen and obviously made recently. Eakin's partner had ridden this way, as Slocum had thought. The proof wasn't needed for confirmation, but it made him feel on top of the situation.

From below he heard Atkinson shouting at his men. The marshal had another body on his hands and no one to blame. Even if he believed Elena Warburton's phony eyewitness account of Ernie Eakin's death, he had to worry that this unprovoked murder was the start of a bloody feud in Leadville.

Slocum trooped along the ridge, then found himself working back down toward town. He had come to a decision about what to do and headed for the stable where he had left his horse. The stable hand snored loudly at the back. Slocum saddled up and rode out without waking the man.

He found the railroad tracks easily enough—they dominated the northern entry to Leadville. The road alongside the tracks was less traveled this time of the year, as Slocum had learned coming in from Denver. He rode north, looking for landmarks shown on the crude map until he found a narrow trail running down into a valley.

As he turned westward, he stopped. A groan escaped his

lips. He had overlooked something important by not peeling the map off the wall before he left the house. Atkinson had the same information he did, though what the marshal chose to do with it was something of a poser. Still wet, the map had to be recently stuck onto the wall. But would Atkinson want to leave town to find what the map pointed toward?

Slocum didn't know. He hesitated following the trail any farther. What lay ahead was likely nothing. He had assumed the railroad tracks and the valley were those around Leadville. That scrap could have been in the boy's pocket for months and meant nothing.

"Shut up, Lem. You make more noise than a troop of monkeys."

"What do you know about monkeys, Marshal? You ever see one?"

"I saw a cage of them at a traveling circus when I was a kid, and you chatter just like them."

Slocum wheeled his horse around and headed back toward the railroad tracks, barely crossing the metal rails when he saw the dark outlines of two riders coming from the direction of town. He sat quietly as Marshal Atkinson found the same trail down into the valley.

"What do you think, Marshal? This gonna get us the varmint what killed the boy?"

"This is out of my jurisdiction," Atkinson said. "If I find anything down there, it might not be legal for me to arrest anyone. I'd have to scare up the sheriff to do the arresting."

"He's never where you kin find him," Lem said. "Heard tell he's always out on a bender."

"I could use a shot or two right about now," Atkinson admitted.

"So, we're goin' back to town?" Lem sounded hopeful.

"We'll ride a ways along the trail to see what we can find."

Slocum saw the indistinct riders disappear down toward

the valley. He looked up, trying to spot his lucky star. If he had continued, the marshal would have overtaken him for certain. Turning his mare's face, he rode back toward town. A smile crept onto his lips as he considered getting that drink the marshal had hankered after.

Let the lawman spend the cold night on the trail. Slocum would be nice and warm in a bed. That thought turned to other pursuits. He remembered the way Elena had brushed against him at the hotel, the way she had looked up, her brown eyes wide and inviting. The taste of her lips still lingered on his.

Slocum left his horse in the livery stable, the stable hand still sawing wood at the rear. As far as the man knew, Slocum had never ridden his horse from town. Whether he would need that as an alibi if—when—the marshal came sniffing around trying to find himself a killer, Slocum didn't know. It wouldn't hurt. And it wouldn't hurt to have an even better alibi for where he spent the entire night.

He went to the hotel and considered using the back stairs when he remembered he didn't know which was Elena's room. Slocum turned to the lobby, where Jethro slept, his head on his crossed arms at the counter. Moving carefully to avoid waking the clerk, Slocum pulled the register around and found Elena Warburton's name and the room number penciled in beside her signature.

The steps creaked as he made his way to the second floor, but Jethro was too sound asleep to notice. Slocum went down the corridor to a room halfway to the exit leading to the back staircase. He tried the doorknob. It turned, and he slipped into the room.

He saw a dark form on the bed and crossed to it. He reached down to touch Elena when he heard a sound that sent a cold chill up his spine.

Barely had the six-shooter cocked when he heard, "Move a muscle and I'll kill you."

4

"It's me, Slocum," he said.

"Keep your hands away from that pistol. I've seen how good you are with it."

"Elena," he said, starting to turn. The pistol butt hit him on the shoulder, sending bright pain down the length of his right arm. He grunted and turned to face her. She held the small six-shooter in a firm grip. The look of determination warned him she was ready to cut him down where he stood.

He rubbed his arm to get the circulation back. She reached out, plucked his Colt Navy from its holster, and tossed it onto the bed.

"You're not afraid to wake up your partner?" Slocum asked, jerking his left thumb in the direction of the bed. When she said nothing, he reached back and poked the lump under the covers. She had covered a pillow with the blanket, making it seem as if someone was sleeping in the bed, while she waited with her gun ready for intruders over in the far corner of the room.

"Where are they?"

"You can put down the gun."

This only made her more determined. The set to her jaw, the way she squared her shoulders, the finger tightening on the trigger, all warned Slocum his life would be over in a flash if he didn't calm her down.

"Look, Elena, I've been chased by the marshal and barely got away twice. I haven't slept and—"

"And you thought you'd curl up next to me? You? A thief and a liar!"

"If you think that, turn me over to the marshal," he said coldly.

"I need what you know. He only wants you for murder."

Slocum mulled over what she said. Elena thought her mission was more important than the local lawman bringing a killer to justice.

"I tracked the youngster I shot to a house on the outskirts of town," he said. "He died and didn't tell me a damned thing. His partner was waiting for him but got away. That's all I know."

"A deputy made a fuss telling the marshal how a man had been murdered," Elena said. "Since Atkinson and his deputies rode in the direction you'd taken, it wasn't much of a jump to believe you were responsible."

"I was, but you were there. It was the boy—Ernie Eakin's brother—I shot. He lived long enough to reach what must have been the meeting place for the counterfeiters."

"Where are the planchets?"

"What?"

"The milled slugs used to make the fakes. Don't play dumb, John. It doesn't become you."

He saw no lessening of her attention. The gun was as steady in her hand as it had been earlier. If anything, she was more determined to find where the lead slugs were. And he didn't know.

Or maybe he did.

"I found a map," he said. "I thought it was to a

rendezvous—and it might have been. It could also be where your slugs are hidden."

"Where?"

"I don't have any reason to tell you. You're as likely to gun me down if I tell you as to let me ride off."

"I won't."

"Then you'd turn me over to Atkinson. That'd be an attractive package for him, all wrapped up in brown paper and tied with a string bow. You get your planchets, and I end up in jail."

"The marshal knows it was self-defense," she said.

"Only for Ernie Eakin's death, and that's because you lied. If you had a change of heart, maybe you didn't see what you thought you had, I'll swing for killing him. And if you don't give me an alibi for the killing you did witness, Atkinson has me for two murders."

"I need the blanks."

"I saw a map," Slocum said, "and I swear I won't tell you anything if you don't put down the gun."

She wavered. He acted. Slocum made a feint with his still-numb right arm and grabbed the pistol with his left. He winced as she pulled the trigger, but he hadn't grabbed for the barrel but the handle. The hammer fell on the web between the thumb and forefinger of his left hand. He jerked the weapon away and tossed it on the bed next to his Colt, then stepped up to encircle her with his arms.

Slocum let out a moan of pain when something sharp went into his right side. He stepped back and saw a tiny blossom of red on his vest, coming around a hole where a blade had penetrated. In her left hand, Elena held a short-bladed knife, now decorated with his bright red blood.

"You're going to tell me where the planchets are," she said.

Before he could turn to pick up one of the guns, she shoved him. Between his tingling right arm and the pain in his side where she had stabbed him, he was unsteady enough.

The push sent him against the bed and then to the floor. Before he could recover, she had picked up her six-shooter again and trained it on him.

"The slugs. Where are they?"

"I'm not one of the gang," he said.

"It doesn't matter to me if you are in cahoots with them. For what it's worth, I doubt you are. They're too clever to ever take anyone like you into the gang."

"Thanks for the vote of confidence," Slocum said, wincing as he pressed his fingers into the knife wound to keep it from bleeding more than it was. He scooted around on the floor and got his back to the wall so he could examine the wound. It was hardly more than a shallow scratch, but he was bleeding like a stuck pig.

"Go on," she said. "Patch yourself up. Then you're going to take me to the rest of the gang."

"So you can arrest them? You're not a federal marshal. What are you?"

"I'm employed by the Secret Service."

"Like hell you are," he said.

"I am!" This flustered her. Incongruously, he thought she looked even more desirable than she had before when he saw her outrage. Slocum had to remind himself she would have gunned him down and *had* stabbed him.

"You're playacting. You ought to be on stage down the street with the burlesque troupe playing at the opera house."

"I am a certified agent for the Pinkerton Detective Agency," she said, drawing herself up as if this gave her more authority.

Slocum peeled back his vest and shirt, then reached up to the bed. She interposed herself. He stared into the bore of a .32 caliber pistol, but it was as big as the mouth of a mineshaft.

"I need some of the sheet to bandage myself," he said.

"Oh." She stepped away, but he saw that she hastily grabbed his Colt off the bed before he pulled the sheet down where he could rip off long strips. The linen was clean—or as clean as he was likely to get.

"Soak this in your washbasin," he said, tossing a fluttering strip to her. Slocum found new reasons to admire her. She caught the cloth in her left hand and never let the muzzle trained on him waver even a hair. Keeping the gun steady, she dunked the cloth in the water.

"Here," she said, tossing the soaked strip back into his hand.

She was as alert as anyone who'd ever gotten the drop on him. He made out as if the wound were worse than it actually was, playing for time. That might cause her to lower her guard for an instant, if not now then later. He clumsily wrapped the linen strip around his middle and cinched it tight. It made breathing difficult, but he was having trouble because of the altitude anyway.

Slocum started to stand, but she shoved him back down.

"You stay there."

"You're not going to sleep. I want to, so let me use the bed."

"We have to get the slugs so I can put an end to the counterfeiting," she said.

"It's not going to be before sunup. The marshal and a deputy were on the trail, but they're not likely to find anything since they're hunting for a gunman, not a counterfeiter. When they're back in town, we can hunt for your gang."

"Well, all right." He saw how she worried over the delay. For a moment, a flash of concern crossed her face, then it disappeared and she became all business again. "Go on. You can sleep in the bed, but if your feet touch the floor, I'll shoot you where you stand."

"Fair enough." Slocum moaned loudly to add to the fantasy that he was badly wounded, then flopped onto the bed so hard that it squeaked under his weight. He considered asking her to join him, but that wouldn't be in keeping with a man so seriously wounded that he could barely move.

Shuddering theatrically, he stretched out on the bed and surprised himself by quickly going to sleep.

Sunlight slanted in across his face and woke him. He opened one eye and hunted for Elena. He heard movement from behind him, but not on the bed.

"I have my gun trained on your head, John. I know you're awake, and we're going to find the planchets."

He rolled over and winced. This wasn't acting; the pain in his side was real enough from getting stabbed.

"I don't know if I can ride."

"Then I have no more use for you," she said. "The marshal will gladly incarcerate you. Did you like his jail cell? I thought it was so . . . confining."

Slocum groaned as he sat up on the bed. She held the six-shooter on him in her rock-steady grip.

"Might be I can ride."

"Might be you remember where we're heading, too."

"Are you ready for what you might find? The Eakin brothers were only a couple of small-time crooks. There are others, and they won't be easily caught."

"You think because I am a woman that I am incapable of bringing crooks to justice. You're wrong." Her cheeks turned rosy as her ire built. "I'm as good as anyone in the Pinkerton Detective Agency."

"You don't have to prove anything to me," Slocum said. This made Elena even angrier.

"I am doing this to put terrible men behind bars. Counterfeiting can destroy a country."

Slocum knew too many other things that destroyed countries, but he saw that nothing he might say would deter her. Whatever drove her was as consuming as a prairie fire.

"There's no good reason to think you'll find anything," he said. "The map could have been about anything. Hell, the map could have meant some valley in Montana or Nevada."

She said nothing. He heaved himself off the bed, didn't have to fake a wince as pain stabbed into his side, then straightened slowly. He could ride but there wouldn't be much chance he could outride her in his condition.

Walking slowly, he went down the back stairs with Elena behind him. She had her pistol trained on him, but she'd concealed it in her handbag and she looked as if she were simply following at a respectful distance. More than once Slocum considered just heading on to the marshal's office and seeing what would happen. The only ace he held in his hand was the location suggested by the map—but if that didn't pan out, he was a goner. She would have no use for him and would probably think he had intentionally led her to the wrong spot to save his partners.

Slocum didn't want to think about what would happen if they did find the spot where the counterfeiters had made their camp.

"You got my six-gun along with you?"

"That's no concern of yours. All you need to know is that I have mine, and it is aimed at the middle of your back."

From the way she carried her handbag, she did have his Colt with her. That didn't make matters easier now, but it might if they found the gang along the floor of the valley.

Slocum took his time saddling his mare. The pain in his side abated, but he wasn't going to be able to make any quick movement without feeling it. Many was the time he'd been wounded worse than this, but he had some obligation to Elena. Just what that might be if it cost him his life, he wasn't certain. For now, he would ride along and see if she was as tough as she said. After all, anyone could talk a good game, especially a lovely woman claiming to be a Pinkerton detective.

He rode parallel to the railroad tracks, then cut down toward the valley when he heard a train coming.

"Don't get any ideas," Elena said. "My horse isn't going to be spooked by the train. Not the rumble of the wheels or the whistle blast."

Slocum looked from her down the trail. The mud had

gobbled up the tracks from the prior night. The hoofprints might have frozen in the mud as Eakin's partner rode down followed by the marshal and his deputy, but the springtime sun had taken the chill off and turned the icy slush to hoof-deep mud.

"Is this where the map showed?"

"It is," Slocum said. He drew rein and turned to her, looking her square in the eye. "If I was one of the gang, why'd I need a map? I'd know where to rendezvous."

"Not if you were a hireling," she said. "You can make the same argument about Ernie Eakin and his brother. Why'd they have a map if they were part of the gang?"

"There's a reason they chose this for a campsite, if they're even here," Slocum said. "We'll be exposed all the way to the valley floor. If there's a lookout, he'll spot us for certain before we're halfway down."

"I'll take that chance," she said. "After all, you're riding in front of me. If you're one of the gang, they're more inclined to let us pass."

"And if I'm not, I get shot first being your shield."

"I don't see that as a flaw in the plan," she said. "Now ride."

He started down the steep trail, letting his horse pick her way in the mud-slick ground. More than once his horse stumbled but he saw no reason to dismount and walk the horse down. The mare was more surefooted than he was.

Slocum kept an eye peeled for anyone below along the valley floor. He doubted Marshal Atkinson and his deputy had gone all the way down. From the way they'd been arguing, Lem would have surely returned to town. Likely the marshal wouldn't have been far behind if he hadn't joined him right away. This was miles out of Leadville jurisdiction, and Atkinson wasn't inclined to call in the sheriff or a federal marshal. That would make him look foolish and incompetent, and more than this, Slocum doubted the marshal thought much in the way of a crime had been committed. Men died every day in the mines. Having a street sneak thief gunned down hardly mattered. More likely, Atkinson would have been mightily upset if one of the horse owners from the racetrack a mile south of town had been killed. That would cause a public outcry. But the death of a pan-handler?

"You see anybody moving around down below?" Slocum called over his shoulder.

"I'm watching you," Elena said. The strain in her voice told him how hard the going was for her horse.

"If you like, we can dismount and walk our horses."

"You just want me on foot so you can get away."

Slocum snorted. The trail was hardly wider than his shoulders, sloped downward steeply, and had an inch-deep layer of mud in the good places. The only way to escape fast would be to step over the brink and fall fifty feet to where the road switched back lower on the valley side.

Fifteen minutes passed and the sun was almost directly overhead. Slocum's belly growled from lack of food, and his canteen was almost empty. To make matters worse, he saw the glint of sunlight off polished metal below.

"Why are you stopping? Keep going. I want to reach the valley bottom before my horse collapses under me."

"There. See it?" Slocum pointed. He looked back and saw Elena wasn't following the line of his arm and finger. He stabbed out more emphatically, and she finally looked. She caught her breath. "There's at least three men down there, about where the trail feeds out into the valley. They're waiting for us."

"Do you know them?"

"I told you before, I just got into town. I'm not riding with any gang, much less those owlhoots."

"We can't retreat. Why, there's hardly room to turn our horses around. And that'd leave you behind me all the way to the summit."

"Might be a better view," Slocum said. She shot him an angry look.

"We keep going. They might not be your cronies. Or if they are, I expect you to lie and say I am with you and to take us to whoever's the boss."

"If they're smart enough to have avoided getting caught so far, that story'd never be believed. You've got my gun. A man with an empty holster's likely to be a prisoner, not whatever you'd want them to think we are."

"Don't get smart with me." She chewed her lip. "I can return your six-shooter, but I'd take out the bullets."

"Keep it," Slocum said. "I have the feeling we're going to be shooting our way out of an ambush, and reloading takes time."

"Where'd they go? I've lost them." The hint of panic told Slocum the lady detective wasn't sure what to do next. She was wrong about the width of the road, but that probably came from her uneasiness riding astride a horse. He wondered what other trouble her lack of experience might be getting them into.

"It's not much of an ambush if your victim can see you."

"But you spotted them!"

"They don't know that. If the sun hadn't been directly overhead, there wouldn't have been any reflection off their gun barrels. Might be the sun's past zenith now, and that's why they vanished."

"Or they intend to shoot us as we ride out."

Slocum rubbed his leg back and forth across the sheath holding his Winchester. Elena hadn't thought to take it or remove it and leave it back in the Leadville stables. The rifle might prove more useful than a hand gun when the fighting started. And Slocum had no doubt that it would.

"Here," she said, riding closer so her horse brushed up against the flank of Slocum's mare. Left-handed, she awkwardly pulled his Colt from her purse and tossed it to him.

He caught it in both hands to keep from dropping it into the mud. A twinge cut through his side, reminding him of his limitations.

"Why'd you change your mind about me?"

"I didn't. There's no other way I can see out of this trap."

"If I'm in the gang, all I have to do is call out to them and shoot you." Slocum held his six-shooter so that it was aimed past Elena but only a small shift would bring it to bear.

"Are you?"

"I'm not in the gang. I don't know who they are or anything about counterfeiting."

"In that case, here," Elena said. She rested her gun on the saddle in front of her and fished around in her purse for the six cartridges she had removed from his Colt. Leaning forward, she handed them to him.

Slocum caught her wrist and considered pulling her off the horse. Instead, he took the bullets and reloaded. Barely had he slipped the final round into its chamber when a bullet ricocheted off a rock above his head. A split second later, the report from the rifle reached him.

"They decided not to wait," he told her.

"What'll we do, John?"

"Two choices. Die or die fighting."

Three more bullets dug muddy graves for themselves in the trail as the unseen sniper worked to find the range.

"I don't like those choices," Elena said.

Slocum didn't either, but he saw no way out of the ambush.

5

"We've got to get away!" Elena Warburton's voice almost broke with fear. She fired several times, causing their horses to rear and kick out.

"Stop that," Slocum snapped. He pulled his rifle from the saddle boot and levered in a round. "We can't see them, but they can see us. Don't waste your ammunition."

"But, John—"

Slocum lifted the rifle to his shoulder and used his knees to urge his mare down the trail. Alert for any movement below, he found several spots where the hidden sniper might be. At the first movement in a bush near a stunted cottonwood, he swung in that direction and smoothly pulled back the trigger. The recoil had barely died when he was doubled over in pain. He had twisted, hurting his side.

The pain saved his life. Three slugs ripped through the air where his head had been only an instant before.

"Missed," he grated out. "Ride faster. Follow me."

"But they'll kill us!"

"Better to take a bullet in the chest than the back," he said, biting back a cry of agony as he swiveled in the saddle. He fired a second time. This time his slug grazed the limb of the cottonwood and tore through vegetation. He heard a loud curse. He hadn't killed the sniper but had spooked him.

"Faster," he heard from behind. Elena snapped the reins and her horse nudged into Slocum's. The plan was to charge down the trail, giving only a moving target. Most men weren't that good marksmen. Slocum had been a sniper during the war and had learned patience others had ignored. Sitting in the crook of a tree for long hours overnight had more than once allowed him to get a decent shot at a Federal officer at first light. The glint of dawn off an officer's gold braid was all the target he had needed. With one shot he had swung the tide of battle in favor of butternut-clad soldiers more than once.

His horse slogged through the mud and picked up the pace when the trail began to level off. This provided both a benefit and more danger. Getting off the trail allowed him to dodge in different directions, even as he galloped. At the same time, the snipers no longer needed to fire uphill, which was always a tricky shot over a hundred yards.

"There," he said, firing steadily as he rode toward a stand of scrub oak. Slocum heard a horse thundering behind him and hoped it was Elena's. Taking the time to look wasn't in the cards. He drew fire from two riflemen now.

His horse burst through the vegetation circling the knot of trees and into a small clearing. Surrounded by trees on all sides, he grabbed the reins, slowed his horse, and then wheeled it around. Two frenzied beats of his heart. Three. Four. No Elena. Just as he prepared to leave the dubious shelter afforded by the trees to find her, she blundered into the clearing.

Her clothing was torn, showing she had chosen a different, thornier trail through the woods. Tiny lacerations had turned her face into a bloody mask, and she struggled to control her similarly cut up horse. She straightened in the saddle as a scream ripped from her throat. Slocum aimed his rifle directly at her—and fired.

Elena threw herself to the side and landed hard on the ground. Slocum wasted no time getting off another round at the man riding after her through the woods. His second shot hit the outlaw directly in the chest and knocked him from his horse. The thud as the dead body hit the ground echoed and then vanished amid the frightened neighing of horses, Slocum's included.

He used his knees to control his mare so he could get off another shot. This raced deep into the ring of trees and missed its target, but the mere act of firing sent the second outlaw running away. Slocum held off another shot to conserve his ammo.

He kicked free of the stirrups and hit the ground. His knees sagged as the shock rattled up his legs and into his side. When the red cloud of pain faded a mite, he went to where Elena lay unmoving.

"Gotta get up. They're still coming. Don't know how many." He looked from her still body into the woods and saw dark shapes moving about. Before he could get his rifle to his shoulder, he heard movement. Elena rolled over and aimed her six-gun directly for his head. Her grip had been firm the other times he had peered down the bore of her gun, but not now. Her hand shook so much she reached out and steadied the six-shooter with both hands. She still shook.

"You missed," she said.

"Didn't. Got him. He was less than twenty feet behind you and would have shot you in the back."

New fire past him sent Slocum diving forward to land prone on the ground where he could get off three more shots. He tried for a fourth, but the magazine had gone empty on him.

"Got to get a box of cartridges from my saddlebags," he said.

"You shot at me."

"I hit *him*." Slocum stabbed at the air with his empty rifle at the body sprawled a few yards away.

Before Elena could say a word, he laid his rifle down, got his feet under him, and ran forward in a crouch. He crashed into the ground when a bullet tore through the brim of his hat, but he grabbed and got the fallen man's rifle. Prying it loose from hands clutched in the rictus of death proved harder than he'd anticipated. He jerked hard, half rolled the man over, and put his finger over the lifeless one curled on the trigger to get off a shot that hit a man coming through the woods on foot.

"Son of a bitch. Hit me in the leg! Help me, dammit. Help me!"

The wounded man hobbled back out of sight, giving Slocum time enough to wrench the rifle free. He took several more wild shots into the woods to keep their attackers on the run, then he sagged down. The fight had taken all the starch out of him. Side throbbing and too weak to sit up, Slocum forced himself to roll over and face Elena. It didn't surprise him that she had the drop on him.

"Either shoot me or put that away," he said. He was tired of her not trusting him. Eventually her finger would slip and put him put of his misery. Either that or she had to believe he knew nothing of the gang of counterfeiters.

"You're in cahoots with them," she said. Her confidence had fled and her eyes were wide with fear. "There's no other explanation."

"No reason for them to want to kill me, too?" Slocum pulled off his hat and thrust his middle finger through the .45 caliber hole in the brim. "Another couple inches to the right and a hunk of lead would have blown my brains all over the forest."

"You knew they were here, and you led me into a trap."

"Settle down and think," he said. Using the rifle as a support, he levered himself to a sitting position. Then he used the rifle as a cane to get to his feet. A quick glance into the woods failed to reveal any sniper willing to take a pot-shot at him.

"You know where their camp is?"

"It's not too far off or they wouldn't have been so deter-mined to kill us—to kill *both* of us." He hobbled around and let a bout of dizziness pass. Walking renewed his strength.

"It was on the map?"

"All I saw on a map mostly turned to pulp was a dotted line leading to this valley. Whatever's here is anyone's guess."

"I—" Elena turned and stamped her foot. Her horse bolted and trotted off across the clearing.

"I'll fetch it," Slocum said. He whistled and his mare obediently trotted over. The gunfight had spooked her but not as much as it had Elena's horse.

"You'll stay right here. I don't trust you!" She pointed her six-shooter at him again, but the wildness was fading in her eyes and Slocum doubted she would shoot him in cold blood.

"Be right back," he said, gingerly mounting. He looked down at her. "Don't go anywhere." He laughed as she sput-tered angrily, then galloped across the glade to retrieve her horse. Halfway across, he saw a man duck back into the woods to his left. Slocum veered from where Elena's horse had come to a halt for a patch of juicy grass and galloped toward the man on foot.

Elena screamed in fury at him, but Slocum saw the man rise from the woods, draw his six-gun, and start to fire. Re-alizing Slocum presented too difficult a target, the man darted back into the woods. As Slocum reached the edge of the clearing, he heard hoofbeats going away. He maneuvered through the trees and came out on the far side to see the rider, head down and riding hellbent for leather, to the south. He rode deeper into the valley, about where Slocum had imagined an X might have been on the water-soaked map.

Elena's shouts fading behind him, he tore off after the horseman. He had no idea how many of the gang he faced, but after the skirmish, he knew there was at least one fewer to throw lead in his direction. If he cut this one out from the herd, he would probably reduce the number by half. From the start of the ambush, he doubted more than four snipers had fired on him and Elena.

He snorted as he thought about the woman. She was pretty and determined, but she needed some sense knocked into her thick skull. However she had gotten the idea that he was part of the gang, it wasn't going to be easy to change it. Evidence piled high that he was as likely to have been gunned down as she was, probably because the counterfeiters thought he was a Pinkerton Detective Agency operative, too, since he rode with her. The crooks weren't dimwits and had to know the Pinkertons were after them. Elena hadn't made much of an effort in Leadville to keep from being noticed. If one of the Eakins hadn't mentioned her to their boss, someone else in the gang would have. Elena stood out and hardly made an attempt to do her detective work in secret.

Slocum slowly closed the gap between him and the fleeing outlaw. More than once the man looked back and used his reins to whip his horse to greater speed, but to no avail. His horse tired rapidly.

"Give up," Slocum shouted. "I'm not the law, but you tried to bushwhack me."

"Go to hell," drifted back on the wind.

Slocum hefted the captured rifle, but it was empty. So was his Winchester. He drew his Colt, but the range was too great for a pistol, even if both he and his target hadn't been bobbing up and down on racing horses.

He contented himself with drawing closer, but the other rider had different ideas and suddenly veered toward the center of the valley where a river meandered. They hit a grassy meadow, but the outlaw veered again, going away from the river when Slocum came within a hundred yards of him.

Slocum wondered what the man had been thinking. Cross

the river and get away? It would have taken him as long to cross as it would Slocum. That gained nothing except further tiring his horse. Slocum had shown his was more rested and able to overtake him.

Drawing rein, Slocum looked at the far bank and knew the reason for the outlaw's path. A campfire's dying embers sent feeble wisps of smoke into the air. Logs had been piled up to make a knee-high fort, as if someone had thought to defend the camp. From what? The Utes were off on reservations far from their beloved Shining Mountains. No road came down this valley, and the few signs of mining convinced Slocum they had petered out a long time back.

He came to a quick decision and let the rider head in the other direction. Approaching the river, Slocum judged the current and depth, then walked his horse slowly along the bank until he saw where other horses had churned up the mud recently—as recently as the morning. He turned and looked back toward the trail coming down into the valley from the railroad tracks above. A man with good eyes or a spyglass could spot travelers in jig time and be waiting to ambush them before they got halfway down.

Which was exactly what Slocum thought had happened. He and Elena had been spotted, and the outlaws had ridden to gun them down. At this distance, it wouldn't have been possible for the men to know who came after them—that someone did was good enough.

Slocum snorted as he realized he had gone along with Elena's notion that they were after her gang of counterfeiters. Colorado wasn't the most law-abiding state in the Union. They might have stirred up a nest of rustlers or train robbers or any of a dozen other breeds of outlaw.

There was one way to find out. He urged his horse forward into the river at the spot where others had crossed recently. The horse balked as the cold water from high mountain runoff swirled around her legs. Then it was Slocum's turn to shiver as the water worked its way up his legs. Horse and rider worked their way toward the middle of the river, where Slocum was relieved to find that it was hardly mid-thigh on him. In a few minutes, the horse scrambled to the other side. The outlaws had found a good ford, because Slocum doubted the fast-running river was this shallow anywhere else nearby.

He dismounted and took the time to pour the water from his boots. The hot afternoon sun rapidly dried his clothes but the boots would take a while longer. He worried more about his horse and spent a few minutes wiping her down. The horse still shivered but the spring sunlight took care of any chill before he started walking for the small fort made from logs.

Slocum drew his six-shooter as he got close enough to smell the wood smoke. He scouted the area and saw no one near the camp. He still approached cautiously because he couldn't see behind the logs piled three high just beyond the fire.

As he reached the wood wall to peer over it, motion from the corner of his eye sent him diving forward. He vaulted the logs, hit the ground, spun about, and used the low wall to good advantage. Slugs ripped into the wood. If he remained behind, he was safe from anything but a mountain howitzer.

A slot had been left, probably for the defenders to peer out. Slocum used it to see a man crouched near a tumble of rocks fifty yards distant. Slocum would have put his camp in those rocks for greater security, but he suspected the outlaws wanted to be close to the river so they wouldn't have to lug water as far. This tiny fort was their compromise between safety and laziness.

"Give up. Throw up your hands, come out, and I'll let you go. Don't care if you're tryin' to steal from us!"

Slocum frowned. The man sounded as if valuables had been left here. He scooted around and saw an iron box half buried at the vee of the piled logs.

"All right," Slocum shouted. "I don't want trouble. I'm

just passing through." He tried to open the box to see what it contained, but it had been wedged under the logs and required some work to get it free. A fusillade ripping away splinters just above his head convinced him he didn't have time. Being this near the box had probably provoked the man in the rocks to give up his lying ways about letting Slocum go free.

"What's in the box? That what you're willing to kill me over?"

As he spoke, he wiggled along to get to the far end of the vee of logs so he could peer around. He saw the man going crazy. He stood and fired wildly at the idea the box had been uncovered.

Slocum braced the butt of his Colt Navy against the ground, took windage into account as well as distance, then elevated the muzzle just a tad. He squeezed off a round. Then another and another and another so the slugs would bracket his target. He let out a whoop of triumph when the outlaw jerked around and fell to hands and knees, then began crawling to get away.

Slocum leaped to his feet and saw evidence that he had done more than wing the man. He had abandoned his rifle to slither into the rocks.

Reloading as he crossed the distance to the rocks, Slocum heard a whimper coming from higher ground. He picked up the rifle, checked to be sure it was loaded and a round was chambered, then went hunting.

He found the man sprawled over a large rock. Blood leaked out from under his body and puddled at the base of the rock. The mud there became an ugly mixture of dirt, water, and blood.

"Drop your six-shooter," Slocum ordered.

The man moaned weakly. Then nothing.

Wary of a trap, Slocum advanced and used the muzzle of the rifle to poke the man. Nothing. No movement. Slocum grabbed the back of the man's shirt and heaved—and

instantly regretted it. The man was dead with two of Slocum's bullets high in his chest but the knife wound Elena
had given Slocum hurt like a son of a bitch. He stepped
back, then caught his breath. He was a bit woozy from pain
but recovered to search the dead man's pockets.

A half-dozen double eagles dropped into the palm of his
hand. Slocum held them up to the sun, then bit down on
each to examine the depression. A grin spread on his face.
These were legal coins. He not only had gotten back his
original coin but a hundred dollars, to boot.

Nothing else in the outlaw's pockets proved of any interest. Unlike the Eakin boy, this outlaw didn't have any
map. But then Slocum hardly needed it since he knew what
was in the strongbox chucked under the logs.

He walked back, only to fight back waves of blinding
pain. It was as if a red curtain had been pulled across his
vision. More than once he had to stop as he clutched his
side. There wasn't any new bleeding. For that he was thank-
ful but the pain made every step a trial. He finally reached
the camp and sat at the vee of the logs. Working his legs up
and over, he dropped to the ground next to the strongbox.

Curiosity drove him now to see what was inside.

As he brushed off the dirt and worked to get the box
from under the log, he heard a pistol cock behind him.

"You're under arrest."

Slocum sagged in surrender. He had reached the end of
his endurance.

6

Slocum looked up, anger flaring.

"I told you before that I'm not one of the gang."

"Open the box. The one you were digging for so I can see what you found so interesting."

"I've killed more than one of the gang. How many more do I have to cut down before you believe me?"

"You're always in the right place at exactly the wrong time to make me believe you're innocent," she said, glaring at him. He wanted to take the six-shooter from her, turn her over his knee, and paddle her. The only trouble with that was the likelihood she'd get off two or three shots before he could even stand, much less reach her. She had stabbed him, so putting a few ounces of lead into him wasn't likely to bother her unduly.

"Some men are lucky like that," Slocum said. He wished he had stayed in Denver, in spite of everything going against him there. Or why not ride north into Wyoming? The weather was getting better, but he had decided against that because of the still-vicious winds that whipped across the prairie. Lady

Luck hated him by delivering him to Leadville and Elena Warburton.

"Open it. And do it slowly." With one hand, Elena picked up the tattered hem of her skirt while her other still clutched the six-gun. She stepped away, moved around to a spot where she could watch as Slocum pried up the metal lid.

"I can't tell if there's a lock. Yeah, there. A lock—" He fell backward when Elena fired. The slug ripped through the lock and blew off the hasp. She not only had a rock-steady grip, she had an eagle eye and was a dead-center shot.

"Open it," she said, moving a little closer so she could peer into the box over his shoulder.

Slocum grunted as he pulled the box out all the way from under the logs and dropped it on the soft dirt at her feet. He flipped open the lid and scowled. The afternoon sun reflected off lead slugs. He had expected to find nothing but double eagle twenty-dollar gold pieces inside.

"Why'd they lock up this?" He scratched his head in wonder. "This can't be worth the effort to carry it in a locked strongbox."

"The slugs are the perfect weight and size," she said. "Since they already have milling on the edges, all that is needed is a stamp to make them look like real coins."

"And gold," Slocum said. "There'd have to be paint to make it easier to pass for real coins."

"You know better, John. You put real gold on. Not much, just a thin layer. That way anyone scraping their fingernail over it and peeling away some will think they have a le-gitimate coin."

"Can't say that I do know better," he said. "Is there any-thing around you could use to stamp the coins?" He looked around the camp and saw nothing meriting more than a quick look.

"You know better," she said, color rising into her cheeks. "It requires precision instruments, a stamp, and a smith's hammer. You were taking the planchets somewhere. Tell me where and I'll testify in court how you helped in the investigation. I'm not sure I can get the judge to be lenient, but if you help, I'll try."

"And only get me locked me up for a couple years?" Slocum said sarcastically. It was lost on the detective.

"Perhaps four. Why, counterfeiting will get the ringleader ten years in a federal prison. Detroit Penitentiary will be overflowing with your partners by the time I'm through."

Slocum swung around and sat with his back to a log. He stared at her and knew no argument on his part would convince her he wasn't part of the gang. If anything, he was as much a victim as anyone else being given one of the bogus coins, though he had recovered his original poke. He forced back the urge to press his fingertip against the vest pocket to trace the outline of the real coin, just to be sure it was still his. The bulge in another pocket from the other coins he had taken off the dead outlaw's body would be a dead giveaway to the lady detective that he was one of the gang. Luckily, dirt and his own blood covered the lump.

He started to ask what she intended to do if he refused to go along. Killing him in cold blood was an option, but he didn't see that in her big brown eyes. She thought she was ruthless, but Slocum didn't see the murderer in her. Now was the time to dig in his heels and refuse to budge rather than when they got closer to town and Marshal Atkinson.

She stood a little straighter and cocked her head to one side, listening hard. Slocum leaned over so he could see past her.

"We've got company. Looks to be a half-dozen men, and they're not too friendly looking."

"I've got you as hostage. They'll not want to see one of their own killed."

"Even if I was one of the gang, do you think that'd matter? They want what's in the box, and a death or two won't slow them down even for a second."

"What can we do?" She turned her six-gun sideways and

stared at it as if she had never seen it before. "This is all the ammunition I have—what's loaded already, I mean."

"There's no way we could shoot it out with them," Slocum said. The outlaws were fanning out to come at them from both flanks as well as straight ahead in a frontal assault.

"I—" For the first time, Elena looked flustered and unsure of herself. "I can't let them take the milled blanks. They'll make them into fake coins."

"You think they'd be content with only getting the lead slugs back? More likely, they'll want to kill me and . . ." Slocum let his voice trail off so she got the idea what would happen if they captured her. She turned as pale as a ghost.

"No witnesses," she said. "They might think I know where they're taking the planchets."

"Got to be somewhere around here, but far enough away that they didn't lug the box straight there. If they unloaded it from the train at the top of the hill, it'd take them a couple hours to get it down."

"The last train came through at sundown yesterday."

"That's about right," Slocum went on, watching how the outlaws moved closer, guns drawn and ready for a fight. "They probably intended to move the slugs today, or maybe they were waiting for these owlhoots."

"John, stop them. You know them. They'll listen to you!"

"They don't know me." His words were punctuated by a hail of bullets kicking up dirt and mud all around. The range was still too great for accurate shooting with a handgun, but the gang rode with determination and would be in range soon enough.

"Oh, bother!" Elena stamped her foot, and returned fire.

"You're wasting your ammo," he told her, somewhat amused at her display of anger. Then he sobered. They had to get the hell out of camp immediately, and he wasn't sure the outlaws would let them go on their way, not after they found the lock box open.

"We can take it. That'll—"

"Slow us down so they can overtake us and kill us," Slocum said harshly. He got to his feet and grabbed her, spinning her around so he could shove her over the log wall. The gunfire came more accurately now. He winced as the hot breath of one slug came close to his cheek. Slocum vaulted the log and dropped behind it. He fumbled around for the rifle and found it thrust into his hands.

"Here," Elena said. "You're a better shot than I am with a rifle."

Slocum braced the forward hand rest on the log and squeezed off a shot. He didn't aim for the rider; he took out the horse under the outlaw. The rider flew forward, ass over teakettle, and hit the ground so hard he lay there stunned.

Elena cheered. He grabbed her and pulled her back down.

"There're five more of them wanting our scalps."

"Th-They'd scalp us?"

Slocum didn't bother explaining. These men cared nothing about trophies—other than gold coins. He fired twice more and drove back the men coming fastest from his left flank.

"Get our horses. We're going to have to make a run for it."

"But the planchets!"

"They can stay. You can stay with them, if you like. Me, I want to see tomorrow's sunrise."

Grumbling, Elena scrambled on hands and knees, using the log as protection to grab for the reins of their horses. She tugged, got them moving, and returned to hunker down by Slocum.

"What now?"

"I've only got a couple rounds left in this rifle. Get in the saddle and start riding. Take my mare with you. But don't ride too fast. Just get moving toward the woods."

"But what'll you do? I'm not leaving you behind, John!"

"Can't get the notion of me being your prisoner out of your head?"

Elena started to argue, then clamped her mouth shut and

obeyed. Slocum waited for her to get in the saddle and start riding off before he stood, fired until the magazine came up empty, then turned and ran for his life. He slipped and slid in the mud but always got his balance back. He strained to reach up and finally grabbed the saddle horn. With a strong kick he sent himself flying into the air and pulled with all his might to land in the saddle.

He grunted when he almost made it. He landed behind the saddle on his mare's rump, momentarily causing her to break stride. Leaning forward and lifting, he found his seat. Elena tossed him the reins and then they were both galloping for the woods. He remembered a couple game trails that had angled off from the spot where he had tangled with the outlaw and took the first one since it led deeper among the trees.

"They don't dare come after us," Elena said. "They'll be sitting ducks."

"They would be if we had any ammo. What I've got left is in my saddlebags. No time to fish out the box of cartridges and reload my rifle."

He veered off the game trail when he saw a gentle slope going down to a rocky bank where a fast-running stream gave them the chance to camouflage their tracks. A little. The outlaws would know they had to ride away from pursuit, which took away some of the mystery, but Slocum looked for a rocky spot where they could exit the stream.

"There. Come on, ride, dammit, ride!" He whipped his horse to get up the rocky slope and back into the thick of the woods. If the outlaws rode along the stream, they might miss the point where Slocum and Elena had exited.

Rather than riding parallel to the stream, Slocum cut through increasingly dense woods. Pine, juniper, and oak above their heads cut off all afternoon light. That would make tracking them even harder. More than once he abruptly changed direction.

"Where are we, John? I'm turned around!"

"I hope they are, too," Slocum said. His innate sense of direction told him they were heading back toward the broad green sweep of the valley. The outlaws might think they'd head for the far side of the valley, through the woods, in an attempt to find a trail up into the mountains again. Doubling back like this might throw the trackers off entirely.

Maybe.

If the counterfeiters weren't too dedicated to the notion of wasting time hunting down obviously dangerous foes, he and Elena might get away scot-free.

"My horse is all tuckered out," Elena said. "Can we rest? Do we dare to stop?"

Slocum drew rein and twisted about to listen for sounds of pursuit along their back trail. His side gave him a twinge, but it eased when he didn't hear the outlaws crashing through the forest after them. He dared hope they had escaped.

"We ought to go to ground," he said. "That'll give me a chance to reload my rifle and make a stand if they do find us."

"But they won't, will they, John?"

He looked at her. Another woman might have been panicky asking that question. For Elena Warburton, it was more of a request for information than assurance they wouldn't be killed.

"You've got nerves of steel," he told her.

"Not really. I was mighty scared back there."

"And now you're mad that you couldn't figure a way of dragging along the strongbox filled with lead slugs," he finished for her. He got a laugh, which pleased him. She was far prettier laughing than when she was peering down the barrel of a six-shooter aimed at him.

"What do we do?"

"We're not too far from the valley floor, but if we leave the forest, they're likely to spot us," Slocum said.

"Especially since this is the direction they'd travel with the planchets."

"Could be up the valley," he pointed out.

She shook her head. "No, I've been thinking about this as we rode. If they had intended going north, they would have cut in that direction immediately when they reached the bottom of the trail from the railroad up on the rim. They came this way because their stamping mill is somewhere farther on. We're going in the right direction to catch them."

Slocum looked around and saw a ravine. He dismounted and went to it. The spring runoff had missed this deep cut in the forest.

"Can we camp down there? Is that safe?"

"No," he said, "but camping on the other side, with this as a barrier to stop anyone coming for us, is safe."

"Safer," she corrected. Elena reached out and laid her hand lightly on his arm. "Thank you for not leaving me behind."

"I suspect that's harder to do than it sounds."

Again she laughed, and the sound was musical. She clapped her hand over her mouth and looked around.

"I didn't mean to be so loud."

"The trees and thick undergrowth muffle sound," he said.

Slocum worked his way down the side of the ravine and up the far bank. It took another twenty minutes before he found a hollow where they could camp in relative safety from being seen.

"I wish we could have a fire," she said, shivering. "When the sun went down, it got cold mighty fast."

"No fire," he confirmed. "Even if they couldn't see it through the trees, they could smell it."

"I know. I'm not stupid."

"Never said you were." Slocum looked at the woman through the gathering darkness and saw that more than the cold was affecting her.

"You're good at this detective business," Slocum said.

"Not that good," she said, holding back sobs. "I thought you were one of them. You! You've done nothing but try to help me, and I thought you were playing me for a fool."

He put his arm around her and she settled in, her cheek pressing into his chest. He felt a little throbbing where she had stabbed him, but another sensation began to take precedence. Putting his finger under her chin, he lifted her face to his. They stared at one another for a moment, then she closed her eyes. He kissed her slightly parted lips, and all the rest of his hurt went away.

The kiss became more passionate and Elena turned, moved, came over on top of him, never taking her mouth from his. This suited Slocum just fine. She provided a heady thrill after a day filled with nothing but death and danger.

She rocked back and moved so she straddled his lap. Wiggling her hips a little, she made a face.

"Gun belt," was all she said.

He reached down and disposed of it. Then he worked to unbutton his fly while she watched in fascination. He felt like a snake hypnotizing a bird. When he popped free of the cloth prison around his manhood, she reached down and took him in hand. The warmth of her fingers only added to the heat building in his loins.

"You're as big as I thought," she said.

"You took the time to ponder such weighty matters?"

"Of course. It's part of my analysis. I need to know everything about everyone I meet."

"So you check out the size of every man?"

"No, not that. I mean—" She began to sputter in confusion. He cut off her protests with another kiss as he pulled her close.

He felt her ample breasts crushing against his chest. They ought to be free so he could kiss and lick them, to fondle them and take them into his mouth, but the wind was whipping up, and it was turning colder. Keeping on as much of their clothing as possible seemed prudent.

He ran his hands down and came up under her skirt. He stroked across her silky thighs and moved to their juncture.

She let out a tiny gasp when his finger found her trigger.

"You're not wearing any undies," he said.

"Uncomfortable," she said, kissing down his stubbled cheek to his throat. "And they get in the way. For checking out every man!"

He laughed and then he gasped. With an agile move, she came up on her knees, positioned herself, and then guided him into her liquid core. Surrounded by heat and damp and willing female flesh, Slocum thought he could be happy if he perished then and there. But he quickly discovered how wrong he was. There was more. A great deal more.

She lifted upward just a bit, letting him slide from her clinging center, then she let gravity do its job. She dropped down and took him full-length into her. Muscles massaged his entire length while he was hidden away, and then she rose again, letting him slip out wetly.

He ran his hands across her bare thighs again and around behind her. He grabbed a double handful of straining flesh and began moving her up and down, slow at first and then with greater urgency. Elena gasped and moaned, tossing her head around like a frisky filly as they strove together to build the carnal heat within.

"Oh, John, you make me weak all over." She turned from side to side, clutching fiercely at him with her strong inner muscles. Slocum almost lost control then. "I want you so!"

He began massaging her rump like twin lumps of dough, pushing and pulling, and then his finger found a spot that caused her to sit upright. Her eyes widened. He waited for her to say something. When she didn't, he explored more.

And this set her off. Her hips exploded in a frenzy of movement. She rose and fell around him, then began a twisting motion that threatened to burn him to a fleshy nub from the friction. He had to hold her with both arms when she gasped and began to shake all over. Throughout her release he held her and then she settled down, still around him.

"More," she gasped out. "I want more."

"Greedy bitch," he said, kissing her.

She made no effort to stop him as he sat upright, then bent forward and rearranged her legs on either side of his body. He was now atop her, her legs wide and ankles locked behind his back. Hips moving, slowly at first and then with greater determination, he drove deep and hard. Her cries became muted and small, then she cried out as he felt her inner muscles clutch fiercely at his hidden length once more. This time he could not deny his own needs. The hotness burning deep within boiled up and spilled out.

Together they moved until there was nothing left in either of them. He looked down into her eyes and Elena gazed up at him for a second before saying, "The ground is getting mighty cold, mister."

"You wouldn't put up with cold ground for a bit more of this?" He rotated his hips slightly.

"I would, if you could, but you can't."

But he could soon enough. And they did.

7

"Even using you as a pillow all night, I've got a kink in my neck." Elena Warburton stretched delightfully as Slocum watched. The morning sun topped the far rim of the valley and turned her into a vision of loveliness. Then he tried to move and found the same aches and pains she already had.

"I can hardly move," he said. He stood and straightened his legs, then picked up his gun belt and fastened it around his middle again. He practiced drawing his Colt a few times. His fingers almost refused to curl about the butt, but as he walked around and got the blood flowing, his fingers limbered up and he felt as if he could fight his weight in wildcats.

"Can we fix something hot to eat?" Elena said wistfully.

"There's jerky in my saddlebags," he said. "That's about it. I'll fetch some water from the stream." He pointed in the direction of a small creek running nearby. Neither of them had noticed it the night before, nor had there been any reason to since they'd been occupied with other pursuits. He filled his coffeepot with the crisp, cold water and returned. The short trip had given him time to think.

"This was only a rendezvous," he said. "I doubt the counterfeiters have their operation set up in the valley."

"Why not?"

"How much equipment do they need for the stamping?"

"Once they have the blank disks with the milling, it might only take a few minutes for each coin. The stamping is an exacting art, though. It requires a skilled counterfeiter or the planchet is ruined. You'd be surprised how quickly someone can detect a fake coin if it isn't properly stamped."

Slocum knew how easy it was. A single glance was all it took to know whether he had been given a phony coin. That was why he had been shocked at having the bogus double eagles passed off to him by the boy. The fakes were so good they had to be cut open to expose the base metal innards since a glance—even studying the face—wasn't good enough to betray their dubious origin.

"That doesn't tell me why you don't think the gang is here," Elena said.

"The dies and anvil are mighty heavy, right?" She nodded agreement and he went on. "They haven't been in Leadville long enough to haul their equipment down that hill, even if they unloaded directly from the train. And if they set up a spot to work, why lug the equipment all the way down the valley when all they need is to be out of sight?"

"They need a forge to melt the gold," she said. "That wouldn't have to be much different from a blacksmith's forge. A kiln would suffice also."

"They're somewhere near Leadville," Slocum said. "They came down here for some other reason."

"To pass along the planchets without being seen?"

Slocum paused, then said, "There's that, but who would spy on them passing around lead slugs? I suspect the boss wanted the lead slugs brought here out of town so he could kill whoever brought them."

"A double-cross?"

"Eliminating some locals on the payroll is my guess.

Were the Eakin brothers local or had they come to town recently?"

"Why, I thought they were part of the gang."

"They might have been useful for hauling the milled slugs, and the boy was certainly good at exchanging the fakes for real coins." Slocum touched his vest pocket where the legitimate twenty-dollar gold pieces still rode. "Getting rid of the local hired hands might mean they're ready to move on."

"They don't stay anywhere long, but I thought I could catch them here," Elena said. "I left my partner back in Denver and came here on the train, thinking I'd see someone I knew from a wanted poster." She shook her head in defeat.

"We can explore deeper into the valley, but I'll lay you a real double eagle for a fake one that they took the planchets and went back to Leadville. This shootout will have spooked them so much they might already be on the road to somewhere else. Central City, maybe, or Cripple Creek."

"So? North or south?" Elena pursed her lips as she thought. "They could be anywhere, but I have this gut feeling they haven't left. Something big is on tap here, and they aren't leaving until they finish whatever they came here to do."

"You said you work for the Pinkerton Detective Agency. Do you carry a badge?"

"What? Oh, no," she said, smiling. "Part of the agency went into the Secret Service. I'm with the part not working directly for the government or Department of the Treasury."

"So you could collect a reward?"

She looked hard at him, then nodded.

"You have risked your life, John, and certainly have saved mine. There must be a reward you can receive, if you chose to apply for one. When we get back to Leadville, I'll send a telegram to the home office in Chicago and see."

"How much?" His question irked her, but he didn't much care. He'd had been shot at—and she had stabbed him—so there ought to be a few dollars coming his way to pay for his pain and suffering, not to mention the counterfeiters he'd left dead along his trail.

"It will be adequate, sir," she said stiffly. She turned and smoothed her skirts. Not looking at him, she asked, "Should we ride down the valley to be sure they aren't working their nefarious trade here, or do you wish to return immediately to Leadville?"

"I'm a decent tracker. Let me see where the varmints rode off to after the shootout."

"Very well. Should I accompany you?"

Slocum doubted they would run into the gang. He shrugged.

"Very well, then. I shall accompany you."

"You're a good enough shot if we run into trouble, you can shoot it out with them and save us both," Slocum said. He tried to josh her into a better mood but asking for a reward had soured her disposition as surely as milk left out in the summer sun.

In silence, Slocum saddled his mare and stepped up, waiting for her. Elena took her sweet time and then rode past him without so much as a glance in his direction. A snap of the reins got his horse trotting, but he cut sharply southward, across the wide-open grassy area, while she doggedly rode straight for the center of the valley. Slocum looked hard at the ground, alert for any hoofprint or sign that riders had come this way. He found the main road down the center of the valley and crisscrossed it for a quarter mile before stopping and taking a gander at the land all around.

Elena rode up.

"Well, what did you find?"

"Nothing. Nobody's come this way in a day or more, at least not since the last rain. The only tracks I see are from marmots and an occasional coyote."

"What does that mean?"

"I was right," he said, trying to keep his tone neutral.

Elena was a bit touchy yet. "The counterfeiters took their milled slugs and went back to town."

"So they had someone deliver the planchets, killed them, then hauled them back into town? That seems a bit of a stretch to me. Why not just deliver the milled disks to Leadville and not go through this charade of coming out here?" She made a sweeping theatrical gesture to show her disdain.

"Been thinking about that and there's only one real answer, other than wanting to get rid of surplus gang members. Something spooked them. Something kept them from taking the planchets off the train in town." He stared straight at her.

"Are you saying I am responsible for them coming out here?"

"Makes sense. They might not have known you were with the Pinkertons, but if they thought some detective had come from Denver, they'd be more cautious."

"This is a mining town and there are plenty of gold coins in circulation, but not that many to make a big-time operation profitable."

Slocum had no answer to that, but it made sense to him that gossip about a Pinkerton Detective Agency operative arriving in Leadville would have scared the gang. Elena had mentioned having a partner. The gang might have thought a man had been sent and would never expect the detective to be a woman.

"They might not have been able to figure out who the detective was," Slocum said.

"You're saying that you don't believe a woman can be a detective?"

"I'm saying that the gang might not. Or maybe they got bad information from whoever is their lookout in Denver."

"It might be interesting to find out if any newcomer to town was gunned down," Elena said, her brow furrowed in deep thought. "Let's return to town immediately."

Slocum had no argument over that. Before they reached

the narrow trail winding up the side of the valley to the rim where the railroad tracks ran on into Leadville, he saw fresh tracks. From the way the mud was left after the horses had come this way, he guessed at a half-dozen riders. He started to point out the hoofprints in the mud, but Elena already began the long climb up, ignoring him entirely. Getting the cold shoulder didn't bother him unduly since it gave him a chance to work through all the pieces.

No matter how he turned over the facts and looked at them from different angles, it always came down to one thing: Something about Leadville made this a target too valuable for the gang to pass up.

They reached the top of the road a little after noon, and Elena barely acknowledged his presence when she said, "I'll send a telegram." She put her heels to her horse's flanks and galloped off, leaving him behind to follow at a more sedate pace. By the time he reached the bustling mining town, it was almost sundown and the shifts in the mines were changing. Miners poured down the main street, hunting for a watering hole that wouldn't throw them out if they didn't have money for more than a single beer.

He found the telegraph office and dismounted. His body ached, and he needed a drink to cut the trail dust on his lips and the pain in his side. But he wanted to talk to the telegrapher first.

The man looked up from his telegraph key as Slocum entered.

"Be right with you, mister." The telegrapher finished his message, pushed back his green eyeshade, and picked up a stub of a pencil, ready to write. "Who you wantin' to send your message to?"

"I was looking for a young lady who would have sent a message about an hour back." Slocum described Elena. From the man's reaction, he remembered her. He would have been dead and buried not to have remembered such a lovely woman in a rough-and-tumble mining town like Leadville.

"Can't say much 'bout her. I got rules. Company rules about divulgin' such information."

"She sent a telegram to Denver," Slocum said. He watched the man's reaction and wondered if the telegrapher played poker. The twenty-dollar gold coins in Slocum's pocket would double or more if he got into a game with this man. Every emotion flowed over his face as if he were the greatest thespian in the world. The difference was one of intent. An actor wanted to convey his emotions to an audience. This man thought he was hiding everything.

"Was it about the big shipment coming into town soon?"

"What big shipment?"

Slocum almost laughed aloud.

"You know which one," Slocum said. "The *big* one. On the train."

"You make it sound like bullion. It's coins. Lots of . . ." The telegrapher bit his lip and looked worried at what he'd just revealed. "Look, mister, you obviously know all about the shipment coming up in a couple days from Denver. Don't go spreadin' that around. The train company is mighty anxious about it, as is."

"A lot of traffic?" Slocum made a gesture as if he worked the telegraph key. The man nodded. "Reckon it's got the marshal all het up, what with the train coming in tomorrow."

"Day after," the telegrapher said. He put his finger to his lips, cautioning Slocum about telling anyone.

"The lady," Slocum said. "Did she say where she was headed? Back to the hotel?"

"Can't say," the telegrapher said. He turned as his bug began clicking. Spinning around, he dropped into his chair, wet the tip of the pencil, and started copying the message as it came in. Slocum stepped away and silently went out into the evening with its chilly wind whipping off the higher elevations. The air might chill his bones but he felt mighty warm inside having found what he needed to know.

There was a big shipment of gold coins coming into town in two days. He sauntered down to the train station, checked the posted schedule, and saw that only one train was slated to come in on that day—around noon. What he did with this information was something of a poser. The marshal would be willing to throw him in the calaboose at the slightest hint that Slocum was interested in the gold coming in on the train after the death of Ernie Eakin.

Slocum stopped in front of a saloon and took a deep whiff of the smoke and beer fumes billowing outward. His mouth watered for a taste of whiskey, but he kept walking toward the hotel.

His long stride shortened, and he stopped when he saw Elena standing just inside the lobby talking with Marshal Atkinson. He wasn't sure what to do. Then it was too late for him to simply fade into the night. Both the woman and the lawman spotted him at the same time.

"Wait!" Elena said as he shifted, ready to go.

The marshal's hand went to his six-shooter, and Slocum saw his escape cut off by two deputies.

"Hey, Marshal, here he is!"

"Keep him out there, Lem," Atkinson said. He came out, hand still resting on his six-shooter.

Elena Warburton followed him from the hotel, looking glum.

Slocum had two choices. He could fight or he could run. With a pair of deputies, even ones the caliber of Lem, along with the marshal getting him in their sights, he knew both trails were closed to him.

Slocum lifted his hands in surrender.

"Now that's what I like to see," Atkinson said, hurrying over to where Slocum stood in the middle of the muddy street. "I like a man who knows his place."

8

"You don't have to grab a cloud, Slocum," Marshal Atkinson said. "What do you think, that I'm arresting you?"

Slocum lowered his hands and warily watched the lawman, who never took his hand off the butt of his six-shooter. The two deputies took positions so they could get him in a cross fire if he made a move for his own hogleg.

"You need not be so jumpy, Mr. Slocum," Elena said. "I discussed the matter with Marshal Atkinson and he has agreed."

Slocum waited to hear what the agreement might be that included him.

"If you spot the miscreant who is lugging around the planchets, you get a reward from the Pinkerton Detective Agency." The words must have burned Elena's tongue from the way she spat them out.

"Why?"

"You deserve it. You are the only one who has gotten a decent look at him—at them. I have informed the marshal about my position as detective and he has agreed to aid in my investigation."

"You think the same owlhoot killed the Eakin boy?" Slocum asked. He stared hard at Elena, not the marshal. Had she told the lawman he had been there? Otherwise, he would not have seen the map or known to go into the valley where he had shot it out with the counterfeiters.

"Makes sense, the way Miss Warburton tells it," the marshal said. Slocum looked at the man for any hint he was being sarcastic or stringing Elena along for his own purposes.

"How much?"

"The reward?" Elena looked even more disgusted that he would think of such a thing when there were outlaws to be captured. "Five hundred dollars. But every last one of the gang must be arrested before any reward is granted."

"How many are in the gang?" Slocum asked.

"Why, I don't know," Elena said, her eyes going wide. For the first time a smile crept to her lips as she realized her company might never have to pay, no matter how many counterfeiters were brought to justice.

Slocum wasn't in this for the reward, and from the way Elena was acting, he wasn't sure he ought to stay in Leadville one minute longer than necessary. But he knew something the woman didn't—or thought he did. Gold being shipped into town on the train in two days was a plum waiting to be picked. The only reason the counterfeiters would stay here after all the trouble they'd run into, thanks to John Slocum, rode in that train.

He didn't understand why counterfeiters were interested in stealing actual coins, but there might be opportunities opening for him if he found out.

"Don't go leaving town for a while, Slocum," the marshal said. "In case I need to talk to you more about the gang."

"I'm sure Miss Warburton has told you everything," Slocum said.

"That she has, but it might not be everything *you* know." Atkinson gestured and his two deputies fell in step behind him as they headed toward the saloon across from the opera house, where a fight had spilled out into the street.

"Did you get permission from your partner in Denver to give the reward?" Slocum asked. He saw her recoil.

"I am independent from . . . him."

"Any trace of the counterfeiters?" Slocum made a sweeping gesture taking in the whole of the town. "They came back, and it's not likely they rode on." He watched her like a hawk now as he said, "They're staying in Leadville for a reason. You have any idea what that might be?"

"No, none. I have to go, Mr. Slocum." She tried to keep herself from looking in the direction of the telegraph office and failed. He read her intentions as plainly as if she had come out and told him. Whoever she contacted in Denver was her superior, and she awaited a telegram from him—or possibly another telegram since Slocum doubted she would have told Atkinson the reward was authorized if she had not been told she could do so.

"Reckon I should get some sleep, too," he said.

"Not together, we won't!"

Slocum chuckled at her as he walked off without saying another word. Elena sputtered and stamped her foot angrily, but he didn't look back and give her the satisfaction of thinking he cared. He passed the saloon where the marshal and his deputies worked to separate four men fighting willy-nilly. It didn't much seem that any of the miners cared who he took a swing at. This was their way of blowing off steam after a harrowing day trapped in the dank, lightless mines.

Slocum wasn't sure where he went but he needed to walk, to move, to keep going. If he sat astride his horse in this mood, he would leave Leadville far behind before daybreak. He stopped and listened when he reached the town smithy. The man worked late, the rhythmic wham-wham echoing through the night. Slocum started to walk on, then circled the blacksmith shop and pressed his face against a weathered board in the back wall.

The only illumination inside came from the dull red glow of coals on the forge. He had no idea what the town smith looked like. All he could see was the man's broad back as he lifted a hammer and then rapped sharply with a double blow that made Slocum uneasy. He had spent most of his life around farriers and blacksmiths and knew the sounds well. He was a moderately good metal worker himself and appreciated the color of the heated iron and the sound it made when you hammered it into shape.

The sound was wrong. Not greatly so, but enough to make Slocum look back through the crack and try to figure out what bothered him.

He jerked away when someone passed in front of his spy hole, not inches on the other side of the wall.

"About done?"

"A dozen left," came a husky voice that Slocum recognized as belonging to the man who had been with the Eakin boy when he died. "Won't take but another half hour."

"You ought to work faster."

"This is the hardest part. If I screw it up, the slug's wasted."

"All right," the other man said grudgingly. "Them lead coins are more trouble than they're worth getting here."

"We'd have even more work to do if they weren't already milled."

Slocum chanced a look again as the man with his back turned used tongs to pull a glowing disk from the fire and place it in a die sitting on the anvil. He carefully placed a large cylinder over the die, then rapped sharply twice before pulling away the cylinder and dumping the coin into a bucket of water. The second man reached in and pulled it out, tossing it from hand to hand because it was still warm.

"Looks good," the assistant said, holding it up to examine it by the light from the coals.

"Of course it's good. I struck it."

"Needs gold on it. Should I get some gold paint?"

They both laughed, then the man at the forge said, "We'll take care of that soon enough to make us all rich."

He returned to his work. Slocum backed away and considered what he ought to do. If there were only the two men in the smithy, he could get the drop on them and march them right on down to the jailhouse. A five-hundred-dollar reward would be mighty fine riding in his pocket, even if the Pinkerton Detective Agency paid in scrip.

Going to the side of the building, he glanced around and saw two saddled horses and a pack animal, probably a mule, hidden in deep shadow. It wouldn't be the work of a moment to capture the counterfeiters. Then Slocum reconsidered. The marshal wasn't all that sure about Slocum and would likely suspect the worst of him delivering two men who would declare their innocence. Better to let the lawman catch the outlaws in the act.

Slocum walked softly, making sure he didn't get his foot stuck in any mud that might cause a sucking, betraying sound. When he reached the middle of the main street, he walked quickly back to the saloon where Atkinson and his two deputies shared a smoke with a man gussied up like a tinhorn gambler. The marshal flicked his cigarette into the mud when Slocum went up to him.

"What can I do for you, Slocum?"

"Thought you might want to catch the counterfeiters in the act."

Atkinson frowned, then rested his hand on his sidearm.

"You just got into town and already you're willing to accuse somebody?"

"They're down at the blacksmith's hammering out the fake coins right now."

"You'd better not be lying to me." To his deputies he said, "Come on. Bring your shotguns, in case we run into a passel of the gents."

Slocum hung back, but Atkinson stopped and motioned for him.

"You can drink your fill later. I might not go to the right blacksmithy."

"There's more than one in Leadville?"

"No."

Slocum led the way, aware that the marshal's hand remained on the butt of his six-shooter in case he had to use the weapon in a hurry. He slowed and pointed to the dark building.

"In there."

"Lem, around back, in case they try to bust through the back wall and escape. Sid, you back me up with that scattergun of yours." Atkinson drew his six-gun and looked pointedly at Slocum. "You stay right here, just like you put down roots. I don't want to have to come looking for you later."

With that, the marshal and his deputy sneaked up to the doors. Atkinson grabbed the latch of one of the double doors, then heaved. The deputy surged into the building, yelling at the top of his lungs. Only a step behind, the marshal vanished into the black maw. Slocum waited for gunshots. None came. Nor were there any shouts.

He caught his breath as Atkinson and the deputy came from the smithy.

"Ain't nobody in there. You funnin' us, Slocum?" asked the deputy.

"They were in there. Two of them. One used a die and hammer to pound out the coins and the other—"

"Go see for yourself."

Slocum did as the marshal told him. He went inside and looked around. The interior was still hot from the fire. The coals had burned low but glowed a dull red. From where he had watched, the coals hadn't been stoked to blazing anyway. They might have cooled if the two counterfeiters had left the instant Slocum went for the marshal. He poked around, then knelt and picked up a half-slug and held it out for the marshal.

"So? It's a hunk of lead."

"It's got a milled edge."

"Not so much," Atkinson said, running his callused thumb along the edge. "Leon might use this for any number of things."

"Is Leon the blacksmith?" Slocum asked.

"He is. You think he was in here? You said you didn't get a good look at the men."

"I heard them talking about making counterfeit coins. Is that something Leon would do?"

"Let's go ask." Atkinson flipped the bent hunk of lead and tipped his head in the direction of the doorway. Slocum preceded the lawman, aware that, although Atkinson had put his six-shooter back in its holster, his hand again rested on the butt.

The two deputies walked together whispering and snickering. Slocum followed them with the marshal close behind. A hundred yards down the road, Lem stopped in front of a dark house.

"I hate like hell to wake Leon since he's got a temper, but there's no way around it, now is there, Slocum?" The marshal shoved him toward the front door and reached around to rap loudly. The echo throughout the house would have been enough to awaken the dead.

Slocum heard mumbling inside and a woman's querulous voice. A minute later a burly man wearing long johns opened the door, still rubbing sleep from his eyes.

"You better have good reason. Me 'n' the missus just got to bed."

"Leon, you been in your forge tonight?"

"Till suppertime. When was that? Three-four hours back?"

"But you haven't been there yourself since then?"

"Course not."

"Did you tell anyone they could use your equipment?" Slocum asked.

"Hell, no. Last time I did that, Sookie Clark went and

ruined the temper of my best hammer. Busted the danged thing when I went to use it next. I learned my lesson." Leon squinted over his shoulder as a stream of invective came from inside the house. "The missus don't ever let me fergit it cost twenty dollars to replace that hammer, and Sookie skipped town rather 'n pay up."

"I remember Sookie," the marshal said. "So you learned not to let anyone else use your equipment?"

"If you got somethin' to say, Marshal, spit it out." Leon hesitated, glared at Atkinson, then said, "Didn't think so." He slammed the door so hard the windows rattled, leaving Slocum and Atkinson staring at each other.

"Leon might be many things, but he's not a liar. If he said he didn't let anyone use his forge tonight, he didn't."

"He said he'd been home since sundown. Any of the counterfeiters could have snuck in when he left and—"

"And nothing, Slocum. You might want to impress that pretty little filly with your detective skills, but it doesn't cut the mustard with me. Bother me again and I'll throw your ass in jail."

Atkinson motioned to his deputies to return to town. Even from the outskirts, the boisterous music and loud cries were audible. The center of Leadville was lit up with gas lamps and miners walking around with their miner's lamps strapped to their heads.

Slocum stood in the road outside the blacksmith's house, wondering if Leon was a liar or merely a man in a hurry to get home to dinner and his wife.

It didn't matter. The counterfeiters had skedaddled and had made Slocum look like a fool. That didn't set well with him. Not at all.

9

Slocum spent the next day prowling Leadville and trying not to be too obvious. More than once he saw Lem or the other deputy, Sid, trailing him, watching him just as he was on the lookout for the counterfeiters. Neither the law nor Slocum had any luck.

He spent a good deal of time on the second day bellied up to a bar, drinking trade whiskey by the shot and listening to the talk around him. No matter what saloon he spent his money in, the miners and other townspeople weren't talking about fake coins or the gold shipment due in a few hours.

Slocum turned and put both elbows on the bar, looking out into the long, narrow room, when Marshal Atkinson came swaggering in, thumbs hooked over his gun belt.

"You and the little lady aren't talking?" the marshal asked.

"Not any of your concern."

"Everything that happens in Leadville is my concern."

"Then this isn't, since nothing's happening."

To Slocum's surprise, Atkinson burst out laughing and slapped him on the shoulder.

"Give Slocum here a drink. Not that popskull you serve. The good stuff."

"Why the generosity all of a sudden? The condemned man's last drink?"

"You haven't done anything to be concerned about, Slocum. I know. My boys and I have watched you real close. You had me worried for a spell, that I have to admit."

Slocum took the shot of whiskey and knocked it back. It tasted the same as the rotgut he had been drinking, but the marshal smacked his lips in appreciation as he finished his.

"Now *that's* good whiskey," he said.

"You have any notion about the counterfeiters?"

"Can't say that I have, and I wonder if your Miss Warburton scared them off. Now, I know they were here in town from the number of fake coins that showed up in people's tills. Why, Hector, over there," he said, pointing to the barkeep, "he got rooked out of forty dollars with two bogus twenty-dollar pieces."

"Damn right I did. I'll wring the necks of them snakes if I ever see 'em again."

"Hec, please," said the marshal, "I told you, they're both dead."

"The Eakin brothers?" Slocum asked. The marshal nodded. "What do you think brought the counterfeiters to Leadville in the first place?"

"There's a powerful lot of money flowing from these mines. Not only lead, but there's coal and even some precious metal. Silver. Not as much gold as there used to be."

The marshal took out his pocket watch and opened the case, studied it, then snapped it shut.

"Been nice sharing a drink with you, Slocum. Duty calls."

Slocum almost asked if it had something to do with the gold shipment on the noon train. He had looked at his own watch just before the marshal had sauntered in, and the train wouldn't arrive for another two hours. If something slowed it coming over the pass from Denver, there was no telling when the train would pull into the depot. Slocum had one more of the gut-burning shots, then put the glass down on the bar with a loud clink. The marshal had stopped in to be sure he wasn't getting ready for some mischief—like robbing the train of its gold shipment. Since he had satisfied himself Slocum was likely to stay put, he had left to see about possible lawbreakers in the rest of the town.

This early in the morning, most miners were hard at work, buried under mountains of rock. That made checking on the ones who weren't mighty easy for the marshal.

"Hey, Slocum," the barkeep called as he started out the swinging doors. "You got one more drink coming."

"How's that?"

"The marshal told me to give you another when you was done. One for the road maybe."

"I'll take a rain check." He stepped outside, looked at the sky, and wondered if the perpetual layer of low-hanging clouds was why they'd named the town Leadville.

He walked to the side of the saloon where he had tethered his horse and swung into the saddle. Yesterday he had ridden back a ways along the tracks and spotted a decent place to watch the train approaching. Lem had been his shadow and had never realized that he was hunting for an observation point. Now that the deputies and marshal were elsewhere, possibly getting ready to guard the gold as it unloaded at the depot, Slocum was left to his own devices.

Still, he rode about awhile to be sure no one followed him, then he cut across country, heading north and east to a narrow trail going to the summit of the hill he had chosen. Barely had he dismounted when he saw in the distance a puff of white steam. Seconds later he heard the whistle. He rummaged through his saddlebags for his small telescope. He unfolded it and lifted it to his eye. A few seconds later he found the spot where the steam had risen in a roiling column and traced down to its source.

Without realizing it, he leaned forward, as if trying to get a better look at the train. The whistle had signaled more than its stop. It had released the head of steam powering the locomotive up the hill. Slocum thrust the telescope back into his saddlebags and rode hard, following the ridge. The train was several miles away, but he had chosen well where he would watch. The ridge curled around and finally ran alongside the tracks below. Within ten minutes Slocum was on the steep slope above the stopped train.

"Open up, dammit, or we'll blow the door off."

Slocum drew his rifle but was on the wrong side of the train to get a shot at the outlaws hammering on the far side of the mail car. He heard a muffled response from the mail clerk, then more cursing from the outlaws.

"You should have brung the dynamite with you."

"How was I to know he wouldn't open up?"

"Blow the damned door off. We've wasted too much time."

"I almost killed my horse getting the dynamite back in camp."

"Shut up, and blow the door." The outlaw said even louder, "And I don't care if you kill the fool inside either."

"Wait, wait, you really got dynamite?" came the anguished question from inside the mail car.

The small pop warned Slocum that a half stick had been detonated as proof that they did.

"We got plenty more. You opening up?"

The raspy sound of a metal lock opening was followed by the screech of the mail car door being pushed back.

Slocum heard heavy footsteps and incoherent shouts coming from within the car. He made sure his horse was tethered to a low bush, gripped his rifle, then started running for all he was worth. Airborne, he worked his legs hard as if he could gain traction. He flew though the air and barely landed atop the mail car.

"What's that?"

"Somebody on the roof! I thought Frank was taking care of the conductor and engineer."

"Get to work," came the brisk order.

Slocum got his feet under him an instant before slugs ripped through the roof on either side of him. He used the rifle butt to smash into the roof a couple feet to his left to draw fire. Then he jumped right, got to the edge of the car just over the door, and peered down.

He heard movement inside but couldn't spot either the robbers or the mail clerk.

"I think I got him. Whoever's on the roof is filled with holes 'bout now."

Slocum fired the instant he saw a masked face poke around the corner. Unfortunately the outlaw fired at the same instant. Slocum fell backward, then rolled from side to side, dodging the bullets blasting through the wood all around him. He tried to get to his feet but slipped and sat heavily.

"Let's clear out!"

Slocum flopped on his belly and thrust his rifle out. Three outlaws struggled with a heavy canvas bag. He took careful aim and squeezed the trigger. The hammer fell on a dud. Cursing under his breath, he levered in a new cartridge, but by the time he had cleared the chamber and fired again, the trio of train robbers were galloping back down the tracks. He scrambled around and got off a couple more shots but didn't come within a country mile of hitting any of them.

He swung down, dangled for a moment, kicked, and landed on his knees inside the mail car. The clerk looked half past dead, his face in a pool of blood, but when Slocum turned him over, the man's eyes flickered.

"That you on the roof?" he asked.

"I chased them off but didn't hit a one of them," Slocum said in disgust. If the first round hadn't been punk, he would have dropped at least one of them.

"What'd they steal?"

"They slugged me." He patted his vest and looked frightened. The clerk tried to stand but lost his balance.

"Whoa, take it easy. They clipped you on the forehead. That's mighty messy but isn't all that serious," Slocum said, looking at the man's head wound. "But it scrambled your brains a mite."

"Vision's all blurred." He searched his vest pockets again, then his arms fell limp at his sides as if the bones had been turned to suet. "They got the key to the safe."

"This safe?" Slocum reached out and touched a low cast-iron box with the key still in the lock. "Doesn't look like they opened it."

"You mighta scared them off."

Slocum doubted that. He had taken his sweet time jumping to the mail car roof. If the robbers had the key, all they needed to do was turn it.

"You want to see what they took?" He remembered the canvas bag the trio had struggled with. That much gold would be quite a chore to carry—about as much of a chore as the three had shown with the bag.

"You're in for a fat reward, mister," the clerk said. He looked as if he had gone through Antietam and barely survived. His face was covered with blood, his hair matted, and the front of his coat and vest caked. "See? See? The gold's still here!"

Slocum rested his rifle against the car wall and pulled the heavy bag out onto the floor. It landed with a satisfying thud. He worked the fastener open on the top and peered in.

Bright gold coins reflected their wealth back into his eyes.

"They didn't get the gold," he said, shocked. It flashed through his mind how easy it would be to tie up the clerk and rob the train himself. Then he heard a commotion behind him. He turned and saw the conductor and a dozen passengers. Some of them clutched six-shooters and others pointed walking sticks at him as if they held rifles—and they probably did.

"Wait, Clarence, wait," the clerk said to the conductor. "He stopped the robbery. This man's a hero. He saved the shipment!"

Slocum could only smile weakly when the conductor and the passengers let out a cheer. He had prevented the robbery, and he had no idea how that had happened.

10

"He's a hero. He saved my life. Those men were killers and would have . . . killed me!" The mail car clerk stood on the railroad depot platform haranguing a large crowd gathered to see what the fuss was about. Slocum tried to edge away, but the station agent gripped his arm hard and held him in place.

"Don't go runnin' off," the agent said. "We need a hero right about now."

"I'm not your man," Slocum said, but the station agent made sure he stayed. The clerk came over and grabbed Slocum's hand and raised it high, as if he had just won a bareknuckles fight.

"This here's the one. He saved me!"

"And he saved the gold shipment," the station agent said.

This made Slocum a mite uneasy since he had seen the outlaws struggling with a heavy canvas bag. There had been the one remaining in the safe but he thought the thieves had taken at least one before he had run them off.

"You sure about that?"

Both the agent and Slocum turned to see the marshal with his deputy, Sid, at the edge of the platform.

"Sure as I can be about anything, Marshal," the agent said.

"The crowd's all ready to get liquored up in celebration," Atkinson said, looking disgusted. He motioned to Sid to follow them around to keep the peace. Anytime the Leadville citizens celebrated, fists flew and shots were fired. "I want to look over the car."

"Sure thing, Marshal," the agent said.

"You, too, Slocum. You turn up in the damnedest places." He rested his hand on his six-shooter, as if he was ready to throw down on Slocum.

They went to the car.

"You go through everything that happened, and don't leave out the smallest detail," the marshal ordered. He moved to the side of the car, where he wouldn't be in the way.

Slocum recounted what he had done. Now and again, the marshal looked up at the holes in the roof and then at the dried bloodstain on the floor. He paced back and forth, then knelt by the safe door. He rapped it with his knuckles.

"Can see why they forgot to bring along dynamite. A can opener'd be all you'd need for this safe."

"It wasn't a good idea letting the mail clerk keep the key," Slocum said.

"No, it wasn't. I don't have any say-so when it comes to shipping the gold or mail. That's up to the railroad executives back in Denver, them and federal officials, who don't give two hoots and a holler about such things." He grunted as he pulled the canvas bag containing the gold coins from the safe and dropped it to the floor. He pawed through the coins inside, then dropped them back and closed the bag.

"From what you say, they had plenty of time to steal the coins. But they didn't. You have any ideas about that, Slocum?"

"Marshal, I just heard the news." Elena Warburton climbed into the car amid a flurry of petticoats and ruffles. She looked flustered, and Slocum could understand why. The Pinkerton

Detective Agency was responsible for protecting the shipment.

"Seems your man here, Slocum, saved us all a powerful lot of trouble. He kept the robbers from taking the shipment. Reckon that puts him in line for a big reward." Atkinson looked hard at Elena, who seemed even more flustered at the idea Slocum had prevented the robbery. "Doesn't it?"

"Why, yes, I suppose so."

"There'd be bloody hell to pay if the miners lost their payroll. Last time that happened was nigh on a year back. The former marshal got his head bashed in with a crowbar trying to explain. They burned down the bank and some thought the whole town was going up along with it. Yes, ma'am, your man Slocum saved the day."

"You'd better get the gold to the bank, then," Elena said.

"You authorize the reward for Slocum?" Atkinson asked.

"I'll send the telegram to Denver immediately."

"I'll come along with you," Slocum said.

Atkinson laughed. "I can see why you don't trust her," he said. "But you got witnesses. And the clerk, why, he'd swear on a stack of Bibles that you saved his life and prevented the robbery."

"You sound skeptical, Marshal," Elena said.

Atkinson shook his head.

"Just curious that Slocum happened to be Johnny-on-the-spot the way he was. How'd you come across a robbery a couple miles outside town?"

"Just went for a ride, Marshal," Slocum said. "It was too nice a spring day to spend drinking away it away."

"Wish more of Leadville's fine citizens thought that way. There'd be fewer drunken fights." He cocked his head to the side, and scowled. "Sounds like a dustup brewing as we speak."

"See to getting the shipment to the bank first, Marshal," Elena said.

"Of course I will. That would be a shame if Slocum

here saved it from robbers but I lost it." Atkinson grunted as he picked up the heavy bag of coins and perched them on his shoulder. He staggered a step, got his balance, then dropped from the railcar to the ground and headed for the bank.

"I misjudged you, John. I . . . I'm sorry."

"Let's go to the telegraph office," he said. Slocum looked into the empty safe and came to the conclusion that had gnawed away at him since the robbery.

"What's wrong?"

"I'll tell you when we get away from here."

The clerk led one more cheer as Slocum and Elena made their way past the edge of the diminished crowd. Slocum waved and then pushed Elena through the crowd and back into the street so they could go to the telegraph office.

"You are mighty eager for that reward," she said. She turned a bit frosty again. Something about accepting a reward for what he had done didn't set well with her. And it didn't with Slocum either. He told her why.

"I don't care if you recommend a reward or not. That wasn't a robbery," Slocum said. She stopped and spun to stare at him.

"Explain yourself."

"I think it was a robbery but not like the mail car clerk thinks. I saw the outlaws with a heavy canvas bag that looked identical to the one in the safe."

"But there was only the one bag of double eagles."

"I want you to get an answer from your Denver agent about what was put on the train."

"Mr. Pullman himself would have supervised the shipment."

"Get details about the canvas bag he shipped the coins in," Slocum said.

"Why?"

"I think the purpose of the robbery wasn't to steal the

coins and ride off but instead to substitute counterfeit coins for the real ones."

"So nobody would know they were stolen?"

"It's a better scheme than having a youngster like the Eakin kid swindling coins one or two at a time."

"There was twenty thousand dollars' worth of coins in the shipment!"

"And if I'm right, they've all been replaced by fake coins."

The whistle on the train sounded and then wheels sparked against the tracks as the engineer pulled out.

"The train is returning to Denver," Elena said uneasily. "Nobody checked the passengers."

"I'm the only one who can identify the counterfeiter I saw with Eakin, unless you got a good look at any of them when they were trying to kill us down in the valley."

Elena started to speak, then clamped her mouth shut.

"I didn't think you got any better look at them then than I did."

"So they have the coins?"

"And the fakes are in the bank now with nobody questioning if they are real."

"It'll look as if the Pinkerton Detective Agency substituted the coins in Denver. Our reputation will be ruined."

"Only if we don't get the real shipment back."

"You could be wrong."

"Can you risk it?" Slocum asked.

Elena almost ran to the telegraph office and sent the message to her partner in Denver.

"I can't believe Mr. Pullman would do anything crooked. He is so . . . infuriatingly proper."

"He wouldn't need to be in on the robbery," Slocum said. "The counterfeiters are clever sons of bitches. They make good fakes, but getting them into circulation is hard if you try to do it one coin at a time." He went on to tell her about watching the counterfeiters working in the blacksmith's shop to tap out more of the coins.

"They needed to coat them when they finished stamping the coins," Elena said thoughtfully. "That's not difficult if you can get a fire hot enough to melt gold."

"I'd lay odds that the coins are on the way back to Denver," Slocum said. "It's a bigger town and from there they can scatter throughout the West with their loot."

"Oh, I don't think so. Anyone capable of a robbery like this would want to repeat it. Not here perhaps but somewhere else. They'd use a few of the real double eagles to coat more lead planchets."

"There's never such a thing as 'too much' for a crook," Slocum agreed. He'd had his taste of this in the past when he had ridden with outlaw gangs. Easy money was as addicting as riding the dragon. If the first robbery went off without a hitch, then a second was planned right away. Soon enough, planning fell by the wayside and the bullets started flying. These counterfeiters were successful but had shown they would kill.

Slocum considered the train robbery and realized they were more dangerous than the usual gang of cutthroats. They had needed the mail clerk to be left alive to brag about not losing the gold shipment. Any hint that they had switched bags would set a posse on their trail instantly. As it was, Slocum thought they had simply boarded the return train for Denver and were well on their way to spending twenty thousand dollars in stolen coins.

"Miss, here's your reply," the telegrapher said, pushing the flimsy yellow sheet toward Elena and giving Slocum a look that showed how puzzled he was.

Slocum glanced over Elena's shoulder. He reached down and pointed to the information that struck him the hardest.

"Pullman said the bag he put on the train had been marked 17. The one I saw was 23."

"Why didn't they get this right?"

"They didn't know Pullman's code," Slocum said. "This means your partner isn't in on the theft. Otherwise he would have told them the right number so they could match it up."

"That's a relief. He's an overbearing, pompous—" Elena cut off the diatribe. "It's good that he is still working for the best interest of the company."

"Telling the banker he's got a shipment of counterfeit coins isn't going to help matters," Slocum said. "It's as bad one way or the other. Telling everyone he has bogus coins or just refusing to pass them to the miners—either way will cause a riot."

"I can't let the bank hand out the coins!"

"The only way I see to get out of this is to fetch back the real gold."

"But they're on the way to Denver!"

"Telegraph your partner and let him know."

"He can't arrest them. How would he prove to the authorities that the men with the coins haven't come by them legally?"

"Have him do some detective work, find the counterfeiters, and then I'll take care of getting the coins back."

"You?"

"I have a reward coming. I might as well earn it."

"You feel badly about taking the reward when the shipment was actually stolen?" This thought caused Elena to brighten and a smile to curl the corners of her lips.

Slocum had to wonder at her.

"You might say that," he told her. She took his arm and for a moment he thought she was going to kiss him in front of the telegraph clerk.

"I have another telegram to send. To the same party. Josiah Pullman, Denver."

While she sent the longer, more complicated instructions to her partner, Slocum stepped outside the office and looked around Leadville. Even if the stolen gold was on its way back to Denver, something didn't seem right to him. There was more here, and he didn't know what it could be. Before he had a chance to think harder on the matter, Elena came out and said brightly, "Let's get some food."

"It's a bit late for lunch," he said.

"Then we'll just have to find something to occupy ourselves until suppertime," she said, steering him willingly toward the hotel.

11

"What if I'm wrong, John?" Elena sat on the hard seat, staring straight ahead at a blank wall. She ran her fingers over the outline of the small six-shooter in her purse, oblivious to the rocking train. Whatever held her thoughts, it wasn't the discomfort of the ride back to Denver.

Slocum shifted so he could look at her and also out the window if he chose. The interior of the car was stifling. The conductor had stoked the stove, but the spring weather made that unnecessary when the bright Colorado sun shone through the window. However, lowering the window to the cold mountain air produced an equally uncomfortable result. He wished he could have ridden back to Denver on horseback, though that would have been impossible since the counterfeiters with their ill-gotten treasure had arrived a day ahead of them.

"I don't think you are. The switch was made."

"No, not that. I mean, what if I'm wrong about Mr. Pullman?"

Slocum looked at her, then stared out the window at the tall snow-capped mountains of the Front Range. She agonized over this so much he wondered what lay deep down in her mind.

"I owe him so much. He was the only one who stood up for me back in Chicago with Mr. Pinkerton."

"Allan Pinkerton? I thought he was in Washington running the Secret Service."

"He is. His son, Robert, is in charge of the company. He refused to believe a woman could carry out the assignment, but Mr. Pullman argued my case eloquently and won. He is the first operative to have a woman as his . . . partner."

Slocum heard a different word when she hesitated. She had almost said "assistant" but had changed it at the last possible instant before it left her lips. She had more than solving a case of counterfeiting to deal with. If she failed in any way, if she allowed the counterfeiters to somehow get away, it would be laid at her feet. For all the nobility her Josiah Pullman had shown, he would never hesitate to use her as the excuse for their assignment's failure. Slocum didn't have to know Pullman to know that. If anything, Pullman might have realized how impossible a task they had been given and planned ahead for failure. It was always good to have a scapegoat, and if they—if Elena—succeeded, Pullman could take the credit for not only bringing the confidence men to justice but also for his forthrightness in championing Elena.

"Why do you want to be a detective? The lawmen I've known have been outlaws at some time in their lives. There's not a lot of difference which side of the badge they're on."

"Marshal Atkinson struck me as an honest man."

Slocum wondered. The lawman had taken the bag of coins directly to the bank. If he were part of the robbery, his actions would add a touch of authority to those being legitimate coins. He frowned at this. If Atkinson was a member of the gang, why hadn't he moved on once the coins had been stolen? Something held the counterfeiters in Leadville.

Or the marshal might be as he seemed, an honest man trying to keep the peace in a tough mining town.

Slocum still had most of his twenty-dollar gold pieces left, but he wasn't willing to bet on Atkinson being above-board. He had run afoul of too many crooked marshals.

Elena let out a deep sigh and continued to fidget, not even aware she did so.

"I have a very firm opinion that lawlessness should not be allowed. We should all do what we can to bring crooks to justice."

"Without being paid for it?"

"Well, that goes without saying. I mean, unless you are a professional lawman."

Slocum looked back at her. She had confirmed what he had guessed. Taking a reward for doing what she considered a man's civic duty was wrong. He couldn't look at it that way. He had gunned down several of the counterfeiting ring, and if they should ever get the chance, they'd end his life with the single draw on a trigger. He sat back, thinking about the gold the counterfeiters had stolen so easily. More than a train robbery, it was a clever swindle that allowed them to get away without a posse on their tracks. Atkinson had decided against trying to arrest the men who had held up the train since the clerk had declared nothing had been stolen, and he was basking in the adoration of the station agent and others in town for his bravery. The marshal would have been more inclined to form a posse if the mail car clerk had been killed.

Or if the robbers had made off with the gold.

It was a cleverly contrived crime. And Slocum still wondered if he could turn their brilliance to his own advantage. No one admitted the coins in the Leadville bank vault were fakes. If he recovered the stolen coins, who would complain? The robbers might try to kill him, but they had done that already. Elena would be furious at him, but her position with the company rested on success. He wondered if her innate honesty and loathing for criminals extended to destroying her career?

First, he had to lay his hands on those coins.

"We're only an hour from Denver," she said, pointing ahead. They had emerged from the mountains and were rolling across more level terrain. Slocum felt the engine surge as the engineer built steam and speed. Gone were the steep grades and sharp curves through the mountains. Now any time lost in the mountains could be made up on the flat.

"Your partner," Slocum said. "How likely is it he figured out who had the coins and followed them?"

Elena gripped her purse tightly, heaved a deep sigh, and finally said, "He's quite good at such things. But he might do something foolish like attempt to arrest the entire gang. Without me there to act as a governor on his wild impulses—"

"He's hotheaded?"

"Duty-bound. He might understand there wouldn't be a good case against anyone carrying so much money, but he would bull ahead and make the arrest, trusting the courts to reach the proper verdict."

Slocum had to laugh and not with humor. He had fallen in with a pair of idealists who thought justice couldn't be bought. There were a few judges who would take umbrage at the notion of a bribe, but Denver was a wide-open town, almost a boomtown in the middle of huge mining wealth and showing even more promise as a ranching and farming center. So much money flowing through the city had to be nourished or no one would be happy. Typical boomtowns lasted only a few months, perhaps a year. Denver had shown more resilience, and Slocum knew it wasn't from adhering to the letter of the law.

He sank back, tipped his hat forward, and tried to sleep before reaching the depot. Just as he finally dozed off, the train lurched and they screeched to a halt.

He wasn't particularly sleepy, but it might be a long time

before he got the chance to do more than close his eyes for a couple seconds if Pullman had pinpointed where the counterfeiters had holed up.

"There he is. The one with the bowler."

A dozen men wore bowlers, but Slocum had no trouble singling out Josiah Pullman. He had a lot to learn about blending in with a crowd. He wore a loud checked suit that was a size too small, the bowler sat atop his head as if it had been tossed onto a flagpole, and he wore button shoes that had been polished so fiercely they were blinding from re-flected sunlight.

Slocum and Elena stepped onto the platform and Pullman came over, as if he were on a parade ground and marching in review. He stooped, gave Slocum a once-over, then sneered slightly.

"This is the man claiming the reward?"

"You always carry your piece in a shoulder rig?" Slocum asked. Pullman reacted in shock. "You'd do better to either wear a looser jacket so you can pull it out in a hurry or wear it on your hip."

"Such impudence!"

Slocum stepped forward and pressed his hand into Pull-man's belly as he grabbed his shoulder with the other.

"Draw."

"I . . . I can't."

"The coat is too tight and you have it buttoned up tighter than a whore's—"

"Mr. *Slocum!*" protested Elena.

"Did you find where the robbers took the loot?" Slocum said. Insulting Elena's partner might be fun, but he had his sights set on something more profitable. Twenty thousand dollars was a powerful incentive to not ruffle feathers.

Pullman glared at him, smoothed the wrinkles Slocum had put into his garish-patterned coat, and stepped back a pace. For an instant, Slocum wondered what the Pinkerton detective intended doing. If he tried to throw down, he would be dead in a flash. Something of Slocum's cold determination communicated to him, and he turned to Elena.

"You vouch for this . . . gentleman?"

"I do. He's ill-mannered at times, but he gets things done."

"I've killed four of the gang, maybe more. I lost track. Now where are they?"

"You intend to slaughter them all? I protest, Miss Warburton. They must be arrested and brought to trial. Only then can we find the true extent of this counterfeiting ring."

"Where?" Slocum asked. "Or did you lose them?"

"Of course not. I tracked them to a small house down on Cherry Creek where they were joined by four others. That makes a total of seven miscreants I have identified."

"You see one about my height, wearing a brown coat and with a scar running along the left side of his nose, like somebody tried to slice it off in a knife fight?" Slocum indicated on his own face where the distinguishing mark ran on the man he had seen with Eakin.

"Why, no, there's no one like that there." Pullman scowled. "There isn't anyone who resembles that, is there? You are testing me. You will not do this again. I am a bonafide operative for the Pinkerton Detective Agency and am a trained observer."

"He was trained by Allan Pinkerton himself," Elena said proudly. "Mr. Pinkerton is a master of disguise and observation."

"Mr. Pinkerton's not here, is he? Time's wasting. Show me where they're holed up."

"I have a buggy out front," Pullman said stiffly. "Miss Warburton?" He extended his arm and she took it, letting Slocum walk behind. He watched them and wondered what their real relationship was. Pullman was a stuffy, bumptious son of a bitch, and Elena had allowed as much earlier while they'd been on the train. But she turned meek in the man's presence and stuck up for him at the first criticism. It might be that she felt she owed him the chance to work on a real case, but Slocum wasn't so sure.

Slocum had hoped Pullman was joking about having a buggy, but the small rig stood some distance from the depot, a swaybacked horse in harness looking bored.

"It will be a tight fit, but we can be accommodated if you don't hog too much of the seat, Mr. Slocum."

"I don't mind pressing up against Miss Warburton," he said, just to annoy Pullman. Elena's eyes widened in shock at such boldness, but Slocum was past caring. He hopped up and settled on one side of the buggy, curious to see what would happen. It didn't surprise him that Pullman chose to sit between him and Elena.

The two detectives talked of Chicago and how the counterfeiters were ruining the fabric of economic society. Slocum drifted off, bored with their polite talk, lost in his own thoughts until they rattled through Aurora and then followed a road lower to one that followed Cherry Creek.

"Stop here," Slocum said suddenly. Pullman yanked back hard on the reins. The horse was only too glad to take a rest. For such an ancient, decrepit animal, pulling a buggy with three people in it had to be a chore.

"What's wrong, Jo—Mr. Slocum?" Elena asked.

"It's up ahead, isn't it?"

"You've been here? The only way you could know is if you're one of the gang!"

"Don't get your dander up," Slocum said, hopping down from the buggy. It swayed back and forth as his weight no longer caused it to list to one side. "You don't see that owl-hoot ahead?"

"The gentleman reading the newspaper?"

"He's a lookout. He probably can't even read," Slocum said. He looked around, down to the creek, and then up from the bank to a ridge where another road ran. "They've got a second lookout up on higher ground."

"The man in the tan duster?"

"That's him," Slocum said. "Drive any closer and you'll warn them. I'll go in on foot."

"Why won't they spot you right away if they would see us?"

"It'll be sundown in a half hour. If I follow the creek, the sound of the water will hide my approach. There's likely cover for me to get closer without alerting them."

"He's very good at this, Mr. Pullman."

"Miss Warburton, please. I'll deal with him." Pullman sat a little straighter. "What do you suggest?"

"Turn around, find yourself somewhere to get a decent meal, and wait for me. I'll either join you in a couple hours or I'll be dead. If they kill me, that'll be reason enough for the federal marshal to investigate, and you can tell him about the counterfeit coins and the train robbery."

"You pursue a course where you might die?" Pullman sounded fascinated with the idea that Slocum might get filled with lead.

"Not if I can help it."

"We'll be at the Porterhouse Restaurant," Elena said. She turned to Pullman and said almost apologetically, "I've heard the food there is quite good. You have no objections?"

"None."

Slocum slipped down the muddy embankment to a spot where he was hidden from the house not twenty yards distant. Two men patrolled the exterior, one carrying a rifle. Pullman had found the counterfeiters' hideout. Now all Slocum had to do was get close enough to find the loot from the robbery and take it for his own.

He hunkered down, listening hard. He heard the clank of chains and leather as Pullman turned the buggy around. The man berated Elena for having anything to do with Slocum all the way out of hearing. Slocum had to laugh. They might fit in back in Chicago but in Denver any outlaw could spot the pair of them a mile off. He settled back, tipped his hat down over his eyes, and dozed again, the soft murmur of the creek lulling him to sleep. When he came awake, the sun had set and the night air had turned chilly. A quick look at his watch, its face reflecting like liquid silver in the sliver of moon, told him it was past eight.

Whatever the counterfeiters did inside the house would be well under way.

He tucked his watch back into his pocket, slid his Colt Navy from the holster, and started down the bank of the creek. The swiftly running water hid any small noises he made as he approached. He sank down behind a pile of logs washed onto the bank when he saw the moonlight glint off a lookout's spectacles. The light made it look as if the man had wolf eyes until he turned and paced back in the direction he had come.

Slocum waited several minutes, slowly counting to see if the sentry followed a set path or walked his duty randomly. A slow smile came to Slocum's lips when he finally decided the man was as precise as any army sentry at his post. The instant he turned his back to return to the far side of the house, Slocum moved forward.

He chanced a quick look inside the house through a broken window. It took all his willpower not to cry out when he saw stack after golden stack of coins on a table. Two men smoked cigars and a third held out a whiskey bottle. They were celebrating their victory up in Leadville. They had switched their bogus coins for the real ones, and nobody in the mining town had any idea the theft had even occurred.

It might not be a perfect crime but it came damned close.

Slocum froze when he heard the sentry coming back. Before, the guard had not passed the edge of the house where Slocum pressed against the wall.

This time he did. And his reactions were as good as Slocum's—almost.

The guard swung around and fired just an instant after Slocum. The sentry's shot tore through the flimsy wood wall. Slocum's ripped out the man's heart.

That didn't matter since the men inside were already reacting to the gunfire. They might be half drunk and indolent
but the gunshots sparked them to life.

"Outside. We got company. Blair! What do you see out
there, Blair?"

Slocum guessed that Blair was the dead man. He chanced
another glance inside, and his eyes went wide. The coins
had disappeared off the table as if they had been ice in the
hot summer sun. He saw the last outlaw vanishing through
the door.

He ducked around, staying low, and started firing before
he had a decent target. One shot took an outlaw just above
the top of his boot, causing him to grunt in pain and begin
cursing.

"Get on out of here," the outlaw grated. "I got shot in the
leg. I'll hold off the law."

"Meet us at the palace."

With that, the two escaping outlaws stepped up into the
saddle, each of them wrestling with a heavy bag of coins.
Slocum fired at the nearest man and missed. Then he had to
take cover because the counterfeiter he had winged started
firing slowly, methodically. The outlaw's bullets tore past
too close for comfort.

Slocum sat on the ground and reloaded. The two with
the gold galloped away, shouting as they went. Slocum realized his troubles were mounting. They alerted the other guard,
who had been posted nearer the road.

Slocum now faced two outlaws, one wounded and the
other fresh to the fight. He chanced a quick look around the
side and almost got his head blown off by a shotgun blast.
The outlaw joining the fight brought heavy artillery with
him.

"I'll keep him occupied. Go 'round the other way, and
we'll catch him in a cross fire."

Slocum considered diving through the window and into
the house, but something told him not to try that. Instead,

he found a hole in the wall, got his boot securely stuck in it, and then heaved himself up to the edge of the roof. The shingles came loose in his hand as he pulled, and he had to scramble to keep his balance. If he fell back toward the creek, he would be a sitting duck.

Fingers curling around an exposed beam allowed him to drag himself up to the roof. Flat on his belly, he swung around and looked back down at the ground, expecting the outlaws to come from either side of the house. When neither showed up, he knew he had done the right thing not going into the house. He carefully made his way to the front of the house and saw both men, guns ready, at the front door.

They exchanged looks, one shrugged, then the one with the shotgun kicked in the door and fired. If Slocum had tried to escape by going through the window and the house, he would have been cut in half by the double-barreled blast.

"Where the hell did he go? He's not in here!"

The one he had shot through the leg was smarter than his partner. He stepped back and looked up to the roof. Slocum squeezed off a single shot that took the man's life.

"What happened?" the man inside shouted and came running out, looking down at his dead partner. His mind worked more slowly, but finally he came up with the right answer. Before he could swing around, Slocum called down to him.

"Move a muscle and you'll go into the grave next to him."

"You're not gonna shoot me in the back, are you? You don't have the guts." He tossed his shotgun to the ground. Slocum cocked his six-shooter and waited for what he knew was inevitable.

The outlaw went for his six-gun, drawing, spinning, and trying to locate Slocum on the roof. He was too slow by half. Slocum got off another shot that caused the man simply to sit down on the ground.

"Y-You shot me," he said numbly.

Slocum dropped to the ground, experienced a flash of

pain in his wounded side, then batted the outlaw's gun from his nerveless hand.

"Where's the palace?"

"Wha'? I'm dyin'."

"Where's your rendezvous? Where's the palace? Is it someplace you agreed on? Is that a code word?"

"Sh-Shot me." The outlaw tumbled to his side, dead.

Slocum stood and knew he had been too hasty—and too accurate. He should have left one of them alive to find out where the other two had taken the coins.

12

Slocum didn't want to go into the restaurant. It was too ritzy for the way he was dressed—and that didn't even take into account how he was caked with mud from wrestling around on the creek bank. He saw Elena and Pullman in the front window, obviously arguing. Figuring out their relationship proved harder for him than he had thought.

Josiah Pullman was prickly, dressed funny, and had no sense of humor that Slocum could find. He would be better suited to working as an accountant than as a field agent for the Pinkerton Detective Agency. That he was Elena's superior didn't surprise Slocum unduly since he thought she was on her first big case. From the hints she'd dropped, a lot of promises had been made so she could come to Denver to hunt down the counterfeiters. A woman working as a detective was something new to him, but he had come across a bounty hunter once who'd been tougher than nails but cleaned up mighty fine and even proved gracious. Slocum grinned crookedly, thinking of that bounty hunter and how she had been about as determined as Elena.

Elena Warburton would make a fine detective, but this

mission wasn't going to be what she expected. Pullman would take credit for success and blame her for failure. The fly in the ointment for the man was John Slocum. All Slocum wanted was a reward, not credit with Robert Pinkerton or his father.

Slocum brushed off as much of the mud as he could, then went to the window and tapped lightly. The two were arguing so vehemently they didn't hear him at first. When Pullman noticed him, the man shot to his feet, knocking over his chair. He reached for the pistol in his poorly disguised shoulder rig, then settled down when he became the center of attention inside the restaurant.

Elena put her linen napkin over her lips to hide the broad grin. Whatever she said to Pullman made the man even more furious. He grabbed his chair and set it upright, then stormed away. Slocum went to the restaurant's front door and waited.

"What do you mean, frightening me like that? Look at you, man! You're filthy! I've seen street beggars with better hygiene."

"I shot three of them, but two others got away with the real coins," Slocum said.

"That's terrible, John," Elena said, pushing past Pullman. "Are you all right?"

"They're dead, I'm not," he said. "I don't know any way to track down the two with the gold."

"If you hadn't been so kill crazy, you could have captured one of the other miscreants and questioned him. *I* am quite expert and could have extracted what we need to know."

"Mr. Pullman's speciality is interrogation," Elena piped up.

"I don't care if you cut off their eyelids so they'd go blind staring at the sun, staked them out on an anthill, and then started torturing them Apache-style, you wouldn't have gotten anything out of these owlhoots." Slocum saw Pullman recoil.

"You are truly a barbarian."

"You've never come across an Apache with a grudge." Slocum glared at Pullman, then knew he had only two paths open to him. He could simply walk away, get on his horse, and ride hard to put distance between him and the two Pinkertons, or he could find the counterfeiters.

"Did they say anything that might have hinted where they were headed?" Elena pushed past Pullman and stepped into the street to stand beside Slocum. "Anything. It might be important."

"Sir, you must pay," a waiter said, putting a strong hand on Pullman's shoulder so he couldn't bolt.

"In a moment. I have business."

"Pay up or I'll call the police."

Slocum saw Pullman wince as the waiter squeezed harder, finding a nerve to press.

"Oh, do as he says, Josiah," Elena said. "It'll be all right."

The waiter dragged Pullman back into the restaurant, leaving Slocum and Elena alone.

"One called out to meet at the palace. That doesn't make any sense to me."

Elena pursed her lips as she thought hard.

"I don't know what that might mean either. They must have fortified some spot but without any other clue . . ." She looked up as Pullman stormed out.

"He overcharged me! And the food wasn't that good. See if I ever come here again!"

"Maybe you should eat at the palace," Slocum said.

"You're right, Slocum. For once, you are right. Perhaps I misjudged you and your tastes."

"How's that, Mr. Pullman?" Elena looked from Slocum to Pullman.

"The Brown Palace has a far better restaurant."

"The Brown Palace is where the ranchers stay when they come to Denver," Slocum said, mentally kicking himself for not realizing earlier this had to be what the counterfeiters meant. They had all the money in the world. Staying at a fancy hotel would be easy enough, and they could even get a porter to carry the twenty thousand dollars in gold coins for them to a suite.

"I've never heard of it," Elena said apologetically.

"Oh, you'll learn the lay of the land if you remain here long enough," Pullman said, patting her arm. "But this begs the question. Where did the crooks get off to?"

"Elena says you're a master of disguise," Slocum said. The man puffed himself up with self-importance. "Why not make the rounds of the saloons posing as a gold miner? Let it be known you have a strike in the Front Range, but it's not too big."

"To what effect?"

"You don't want a cutthroat killing you for the gold, but the counterfeiters need a source of gold to coat their fake coins. Where better to get the gold than a low-producing mine? The owner would be eager to sell, but nobody else would pay a plugged nickel since it's not producing that much gold."

"A splendid idea, Slocum. You have quite a head for the confidence game. I suppose that is only to be expected, considering your background. Yes, a disguise." Pullman went off muttering to himself about how he would fashion his disguise.

"He wants to be like Allan Pinkerton. Mr. Pinkerton caught a crook by donning a disguise. That's what began our company."

Slocum waited until Pullman was out of earshot, then said, "Where's the Brown Palace? You're dressed for a hotel that sounds that fancy."

"And you're definitely not," Elena said, laughing. She looked from Slocum to the corner of the street where Pullman had vanished.

"You don't need him," Slocum said.

"If you weren't able to deal with the two counterfeiters who escaped, I'm not sure I can."

"Don't sell yourself short," Slocum said. "You tracked them to Leadville, didn't you? You are a good shot." He reached out and tugged at the purse she held. "And this is what you want to do for a job."

"You really shot three of them?" Elena saw the answer in his grim expression. "I might have to shoot the other two since you won't be there to assist."

Slocum started walking and gave Elena subtle clues, shifting when they came to an intersection so she would instinctively follow, head where he looked, and respond when he tensed as they passed a restaurant and saw a five-story building with fancy stained glass windows.

"You knew the way here," she said.

"More to the point, how do we find out if they are even here? They might have meant something else." Slocum knew deep in his gut this was the "palace" the counterfeiters had named as their rendezvous. If it wasn't, they had to depend on Josiah Pullman actually discovering something by listening to drunks in saloons around town.

"We wait. We stake it out."

"To see if they go into the hotel?" Slocum shook his head. "I didn't get a good enough look at the two."

"You spoke of one having a distinctive scar on his face."

"The one I saw in Leadville," he said. "None of the men I shot at the house looked like him. It's a long shot but worth taking."

They stood pressed against the restaurant wall across the street for some time, but the number of guests entering or leaving was small.

"How long do you think we'll have to wait?" Elena asked.

"You're the detective," he said. Then it occurred to him why so few hotel guests came out. "I saw their horses. I can identify the horses they rode, even if I never got a good look at the men's faces."

His long strides took him across the street, but he didn't enter the lobby. Instead, he followed the cobblestone walk to the rear of the hotel, where a livery stable had been built for the guests. A slow smile came to his lips. If the counterfeiters were in the hotel, they would have stabled their horses here and used the rear entrance. He and Elena would have waited till hell froze over to spot them.

Two dozen horses were stabled here. Slocum walked slowly down the stalls and stopped when he got to one holding a gray with distinctive black markings on its rump. He started to enter the stall to rummage through the tack stored at the front when a loud voice demanded to know what he was doing.

Slocum backed away and faced a well-dressed man.

"This is a fine-looking horse," Slocum said. "I've an interest in buying it from the owner."

"Looked like you was gonna steal the horse." The stableman pulled back his coat and showed a six-shooter holstered at his hip. "Nobody steals a Brown Palace guest's horse. Nobody."

"He was telling the truth, sir," Elena said, hurrying over. She smiled sweetly and looked just a little flustered. "It's that, well, my father has a great interest in horses of this marking and my ranch hand here was kind enough to accompany me here to look for a remuda."

"You want more than one gray?"

"My father owns a quarter-million-acre spread in Wyoming. He has this wild notion that raising such horses will further add to the family fortune."

"I tried to argue him into raising Appaloosas, but he wouldn't have any of it," Slocum said.

"Arabians are good horses, too," the stableman said.

Slocum and the man began discussing the finer points of raising horses. More than once the man looked at Elena as if judging the truth of what she said. He finally came to a conclusion.

"You know your horseflesh," he decided, "but this *is* a guest's horse and you'll have to talk to him about selling. He might be willing, but I doubt it."

"Why's that?" Elena asked innocently.

"He's riding the horse he wants to ride. The man's rich, but then most who stay at the hotel are." He fished in his pocket and held up a double eagle. "Gave me this to look after his horse and gear."

"His partner's, too?" Slocum asked.

"Yup. That's his partner's, but it's not likely you'd be interested in it. Starting to go lame in the front right leg."

Slocum and the stableman argued over the type of liniment best suited for such a limp. Slocum looked up and inclined his head slightly in the direction of the gray's stall and the tack stored there. Elena separated herself from the merits of wrapping a leg and came back in a few minutes, smiling.

"The horse is in good hands," Slocum said, slapping the stableman on the shoulder. "Thanks."

"Good night to you both."

Slocum was sure the man watched Elena as she sashayed out toward the rear door leading into the hotel proper.

"What did you find out?" Slocum asked.

"I took this from his saddlebags." She held up an ornately carved pipe. "How do we use it to find him?"

"Something like that is special," Slocum said, thinking. He opened the door into the hotel and immediately was beset by a uniformed employee, who reached out and pushed Slocum back.

"Sorry, sir, guests only."

"Oh, please," Elena said, batting her eyelashes at the porter. "I know he is such a sight, but it so very important we find the gentleman who lost this. He came in earlier."

"What's that?" the porter asked.

"I found it where he lost it. This young lady saw him come in, but we don't know his name. He rode the gray back in the stables."

"Mr. Timmins?"

"Or the man with him," Elena said quickly. Slocum saw how she angled to get more information but it wasn't forthcoming.

"I can give it to him."

"That would be all right," Elena said, "but this gentleman deserves a reward. You can see the lengths he has gone to retrieving the pipe."

"I'll pass it along," the porter said.

"I want to talk to the manager," Slocum demanded. The subtle change in the porter's expression told him he had hit the target.

"That won't be necessary."

Slocum knew the manager would keep any reward and not pass anything along to the porter, just as the man sought to do Slocum out of his due. If Timmins gave the stableman a double eagle, the counterfeiter probably left a trail of coins in his wake. A reward for a family heirloom such as the pipe might be could amount to a hundred dollars—or more.

"I know the room where he and his partner are staying."

"Look," Slocum said. "Let me—let us—come with you. We'll watch from the end of the hall as you return it, and we'll split any reward."

The porter still thought hard on a way to keep all the reward but half was better than none. Slocum wondered if the porter played poker and was adept at palming cards and dealing seconds. If so, whatever was passed over as a reward would vanish into a pocket, with only half reappearing to be divided later.

"The back stairs. Try not to drop too much mud along the way," the porter said with obvious distaste. Most of his clients were well heeled and impeccably dressed. As they climbed to the top floor, Slocum guessed these stairs were used more for whores than hotel guests. A lingering scent of cheap perfume confirmed his guess.

The porter pushed Slocum back.

"Wait here. The room's halfway down the corridor."

Slocum and Elena watched as the porter knocked. Words were exchanged, then Timmins—or his partner—passed over a few gold coins. As Slocum expected, the porter turned and some of them disappeared into vest pockets. He walked briskly back and held out a single twenty-dollar gold piece.

"Your half."

"Thanks," Slocum said. "We'll let you be."

Elena tugged at his arm, but he motioned her to silence. They reached the bottom of the stairs, where the porter saw them out into the walkway to the stables. Barely had they stepped out when the room clerk rang for the porter.

Slocum and Elena slid back in and up the stairwell the instant the man's attention was directed away from them.

"He was a thief! Why, he was given at least three gold eagles!"

"We're still ahead twenty dollars," Slocum said, drawing his pistol.

"Oh, no we are not! That coin belongs to the Leadville Bank!"

Slocum motioned her to silence again as he rapped on the door.

"Whosit?"

"Porter, sir," Slocum said in a low voice. "I found part of the pipe that was broken off."

"What? There was something broken off?" Timmins opened the door wide enough for Slocum to kick it open and bring the Colt swinging down on the top of his head. Timmins stumbled backward and crashed to the floor.

The other man in the room looked up, went for his pistol on a table. He froze when he realized Slocum had the drop on him.

"Where're the gold coins?"

The man's eyes darted toward a wardrobe. Elena caught the glance, too, and hurried to open the door.

"Two bags, John. We've recovered the gold."

"Good," he said, stepping forward, only to feel his foot yanked out from under him. Timmins had recovered and fought back. Slocum crashed to the ground, then wrestled with the counterfeiter, struggling to roll on top of him since his six-gun had been knocked from his hand.

A muffled shot sounded, startling both Slocum and Timmins. Slocum looked up and saw that Elena had shot the other counterfeiter when he'd tried to grab her. With her pistol shoved into the man's leg, there had been only a dull *fwap!* report as the bullet tore through his flesh.

Slocum used the distraction to his advantage, shoving Timmons off his body and slamming the counterfeiter's head into the floor roughly. Then a pair of smooth arms suddenly grabbed Slocum under the shoulders and he felt himself being lifted up and dropped on the feather mattress. Before he could get up, Elena flopped on top of him. They rolled off the bed, Slocum recovered his six-shooter, and he raised it to . . . an empty room.

"Did they take the gold?"

"No, no, John. It's still in the wardrobe. But we have to go after them."

"Why?"

"They're criminals. I've promised to bring them to justice."

"There's not a whole lot of evidence against them, and isn't recovering the gold the important part?"

"But—"

"They won't rejoin the rest of the gang. They'd be killed for losing the gold."

"The rest of the gang?" Elena looked at him curiously. "What do you mean? Isn't this all of them?"

Slocum closed and locked the door before answering.

"Neither of those men had a scar on his face."

"He's the leader?"

"He's the one I saw minting the planchets," Slocum said.

"But where is he? Where is the rest of the gang, if there're others?"

Slocum opened a door and saw a small bathroom. This was a deluxe suite.

"I'll tell you," Slocum said, "if you'll wash my back." He stripped off his mud-caked coat and then turned the handles on the water tap. Hot, steamy water gushed forth.

"I won't ask you," Elena said.

"What's that?" It was Slocum's turn to be surprised.

"I won't ask until you wash mine." Eyes fixed on him, she began to slowly open the buttons on her blouse.

13

"That sounds like a fair deal," Slocum said, kicking off his boots as he sat on the edge of the bathtub. Elena continued to unbutton her blouse as she went to him. Then, with a quick movement, she pushed him into the tub with a loud splash.

"You . . ." Slocum didn't get any farther because Elena jumped on top of him, causing even more water to splash about. Their mouths met and locked in a deep kiss.

Moving about, they found a more comfortable position in the bath as warm water continued to gush in. Slocum ran his hand over her cheek, down her neck, and then finished the job of unbuttoning Elena's blouse. He tossed the wet garment out of the tub, leaving her naked to the waist.

He bent down and lightly kissed each breast. She sloshed about some more so she could position herself better.

"That feels so good, John. More. Do more."

He did more. His tongue pressed in turn into each hard nub capping her breasts. The throb of her heart increased as blood rushed into the nipples. His arms circled her and pulled her closer. His hands cupped her buttocks and lifted her up so he could scoot her skirt around her waist.

"Wait, John. Wait a minute." Elena got to her feet in the bath and shimmied to get free. From his seated position looking up, Slocum got the sight of his life. The furry triangle between her legs was matted from her dip into the tub, but past this, across her slightly domed belly and past her lovely breasts, he saw how she looked down at him with unbridled lust.

He began to respond. And she saw it.

"Let me get you free," she offered. Elena reached down and began unbuttoning his jeans. When his long, hard manhood popped free, she sank down, her legs on either side of his.

"I want out of my pants," Slocum said, pinned beneath her weight. He pressed into the delightful triangle between her legs and felt her nether lips lewdly caressing him.

"You have to earn it," she said.

Slocum began exploring her water-slickened body, fingers pressing and stroking until he found hidden spots that caused her to gasp in pleasure. A spot on her hip, another on her throat, then he traced over every bone in her spine, working downward slowly until she trembled with need.

"I want you," she said, reaching down to grip him so she could guide him into her hot core.

Slocum lifted himself up, silently encouraging her to peel off his jeans. She looped her fingers around the waistband and pulled downward. His legs were still tangled, but he was free where it mattered. This time when she sank down, he slid deep into her. They both gasped with the gentle intrusion. The water lapped around them, stimulating, caressing, making the lovemaking even more erotic. Then she began moving, rising and falling slowly. He slid almost all the way from her tightness, then delved far up into her tightly clinging interior once more.

Elena added a corkscrewing motion to her hips that drove Slocum crazy with need. The heat in his balls turned to white-hot burning. He gripped the sides of the bathtub for leverage and started lifting himself up to meet her descent. Faster they moved. Together. They moved together until they melted into each other and exploded in sexual release.

She sank forward, her cheek resting on his shoulder. He held her awkwardly, then pushed her upward.

"We've got work to do," he said.

"What? But—"

"You said you'd wash my back."

Elena looked at him, then laughed.

"We had a deal, didn't we? You have to wash my back first."

She helped him get his jeans off, and both buck naked now, they filled the tub with hotter water, turned off the taps, and set to work washing each other until their passions built once more—and then were sated.

"All right," Elena said, sitting on Slocum's lap as the bath water cooled down around them. "I'm asking now. Where's the leader of the counterfeiting ring?"

He moved his hands idly across her belly, then down to her crotch. His finger curled and entered her. She sighed as he began moving slowly in and out.

"You have a way of distracting me from my job, John."

"Leadville," he said. "The man with the scar is in Leadville, but I don't know why. After such a theft, any smart crook would have hightailed it with his partners and be in this suite with a lovely woman, pleasuring her, maybe in a bath."

"Or in that wonderful bed," Elena said with some longing. "This is so sexy, but the bed . . ."

"Later," Slocum said. "He has to be in Leadville for some other reason, something even bigger."

"He needs a fair amount of lead to make the planchets," she said.

"The dies and other equipment he needs must be heavy."

"It's hard to move them around. Some counterfeiters simply abandon everything when they have to run from the law."

"He might like Leadville as a headquarters," Slocum said.

"Why not Denver? It's bigger. There are a lot of ways to escape if the law got too close."

"Or a certain Pinkerton detective got too close," Slocum said, pulling Elena back even more into his body.

"John," she said firmly. "The water's getting cold."

He hesitated, then said in her ear, "The bed looks nice and warm. Like you said, it's a shame to waste it since Timmins has already paid for everything."

Elena heaved herself up and stepped out of the large bathtub. Slocum followed and found himself being toweled down with a big, fluffy cloth. He returned the favor and then they found how comfortable the bed was.

"Mr. Pullman will think we're both dead," Elena said.

Slocum grunted under the weight of the two bags filled with coins. More than once since leaving the hotel, he had considered ways of sending Elena off on a wild-goose chase so he could buy himself a horse, load up the gold, and ride away a rich man. But he never carried through any of the plans and couldn't say why.

"There he is, John." She pointed at the beggar at the corner. "At least, I think that's Mr. Pullman. The one rattling coins in his tin cup?"

Slocum had already spotted Josiah Pullman. The man thought he was a master of disguise but instead looked like a clown in a traveling circus. The spirit gum he had used to paste on a wispy mustache had begun to slip, giving him a lopsided look.

"We've got what was stolen," Slocum said, dropping the bags in front of Pullman. The Pinkerton detective looked up, then hissed like a snake.

"Go away. I'm undercover!"

"No need. We recovered the coins. The real coins." Slocum kicked one of the heavy bags.

"Well, we got back the coins that hadn't been spent. One

of the outlaws is named Timmins, and he got away, but
his partner is wounded." Elena sounded smug but also a tad
fearful what Pullman might say.

"She shot him in the leg while they were fighting," Slocum said, just to watch Pullman's reaction. It was everything he could have hoped for. The man's eyes went wide,
and the mustache finally gave up the ghost and fell into his
lap. Pullman fumbled to retrieve it and stick it into place
but failed repeatedly.

"You shot a man?"

"While they were fighting," Slocum said again. "Hand to
hand. She didn't have any choice since I was trying to bash
in Timmins's brains."

"Timmins. I know that name," Pullman said, getting to
his feet. He stripped off the rest of the fake hair on his face
and stuffed it into his beggar's cup. He looked down, fumbled out the few coins he had in the cup, and thrust them into
his vest pocket, then cast aside the cup with the mustache
and eyebrows that looked like mismatched caterpillars.

"Will you follow up on this lead, Mr. Pullman?"

"We can find him if we work together. Good work, Miss
Warburton."

"I, uh, Mr. Pullman, I intend to return to Leadville. I—
we—believe the leader of the counterfeiting ring is still there."

"Why bring the stolen coins to Denver if they hadn't
intended to divvy them up and scatter to the four winds?
No, Miss Warburton, you are wrong. The entire gang returned. This Timmins might be the leader."

"She'll need a guard when she takes the stolen coins
back to the Leadville Bank," Slocum said.

"Why, no, the coins remain here. I'll take custody and—"

"I'll see them back if you intend to stay in Denver," Slocum said to Elena. "If the bank starts distributing counterfeit coins, the miners are likely to lynch everyone working
in the bank when they find out they're trying to spend lead
slugs instead of real gold."

"I need to contact the home office for instructions," Pullman said.

"Send the reply to Leadville," Elena said with surprising determination. "I'll check in every day or so."

"You can't go there. I forbid it! I'm senior field agent, and you take orders from me."

"Might be she'll only be able to check for your telegram every other day," Slocum said pointedly.

"This is outrageous. I'll see that Mr. Pinkerton fires you!"

"When you turn in your report, be sure to mention that it was Mr. Slocum and I who recovered the gold, killed three more counterfeiters, wounded another, and ran them out of Denver."

"You don't know they left town."

"Then it's up to you to find Timmins and bring him to justice," Slocum said. He hefted the two bags. To Elena he said, "We can catch the Leadville train if we hurry."

He and Elena Warburton left Pullman sputtering on the street corner.

"What have we here? Are you making a deposit?" the banker asked, eyeing Slocum's burden with avaricious eyes. Slocum dropped the heavy bags onto the bank president's desk.

"We need to have a conversation, sir," Elena said. "It's been a long trip back from Denver, and I would prefer to complete this unseemly business with dispatch."

"Have a seat and—"

"In private," Slocum said, seeing how the three tellers all sidled a little closer. Whether they wanted a better look at Elena or were interested in a huge deposit didn't matter.

"This is most irregular," the banker said.

"I need to rest and cannot do so until this matter is settled."

"What matter is that?" The banker looked skeptical, but having Elena with Slocum eased the skepticism.

"You have a vault filled with bogus coins," Slocum said

in a low voice. He didn't much care if the tellers overheard. Since none of them reacted the way the banker did, he doubted they had been close enough to hear him.

"That is an outrageous claim, sir! Such a thing has never happened to this bank!"

"Come on, Miss Warburton. Let's not bother saving his bacon."

"Wait, wait, we can talk. There is a modicum of privacy there," he said, indicating a desk in the far corner of the room away from the tellers' cages.

Slocum heaved the coins back over his shoulders, then kicked open the gate in the low railing and went directly to the vault.

"Stop. I say, stop!"

"We can talk inside."

"There's hardly room."

"Make room," Slocum said. "I'm as tired as she is. She's a Pinkerton detective, you know?"

"Well, I, very well." The banker looked meaningfully at the head teller, as if warning him this might be an attempted robbery. As Slocum went into the tiny vault and dropped the bags, he thought it might be a useful ploy. A bank could be robbed without much effort, no gunshots, no one being killed, if the president simply allowed the robber into the vault under false pretenses.

But there was nothing false and he'd have to wait for another chance to rob a bank using this scheme. Slocum opened the sacks and spilled the contents out for the banker to see.

"An impressive amount of money, sir," the banker said.

Elena shut the vault door. The three of them barely fit inside along with the boxes and shelving.

"The shipment you received a few days ago contained counterfeit coins. The robbers did not try to steal from the train. Rather, they substituted the fake coins for the real."

The banker opened the canvas sack and drew out a coin. He ran his finger around the milled edge, then bit down on the coin. In the dim light he strained to see the result. What Slocum could see in the light slanting in from outside the vault was the way the banker's face drained of all blood.

"Fake," he croaked out.

"The Pinkerton Detective Agency has recovered the real coins—most of them. The robbers spent rather lavishly in Denver," Elena said. She blushed and touched her lips with her hand. Slocum knew that she was remembering how they had put some of the robbers' wild spending to good use. The bath and bed had been gleefully shared.

"Pinkerton?"

"What I suggest, to avoid further embarrassment," Elena said, "is for you to swap the lead slugs for the real coins. No one need ever know you had the fake coins in your vault and intended to distribute them."

"I . . . I've already paid the weekly salaries for the Golightly Mine."

"How you handle that is up to you," Elena said.

"Since we're not returning all the gold, the bank is responsible for the balance," Slocum said. "That'd include the payroll already met."

"I can't tell them I gave out counterfeit coins."

"As I said, this is your responsibility. Now, do you want to make the swap or should I retain the real coins and turn them over to the marshal?"

"Miss Warburton, please." The banker was sweating rivers now. "I need to think what to do."

"The counterfeiter who made these coins is still on the loose," Slocum said. "The sooner Miss Warburton stops him, the sooner the integrity of your assets will be guaranteed."

"There might be more fake coins?" He took out a handkerchief and mopped his face. "Very well. I certainly owe you for this, uh, rescue of my bank's reputation."

"It's more than reputation at stake," Elena said. "Your bank would have been ruined, and you and your staff might have been lynched."

"I, uh, yes."

"The Pinkerton Detective Agency will send you the bill for our services soon. Our senior agent, Mr. Josiah Pullman in Denver, will be in touch."

"I'll lug those out for you," Slocum said, grunting as he picked up the bags of phony coins.

"Everything will be taken care of," the banker said loudly as he pushed open the vault. The tellers quickly pretended to be occupied, but the banker spoke for their benefit. "Your business is appreciated, but you ought to store those, uh, those—"

"Horseshoes," Slocum said, enjoying seeing the banker squirm. "I should have known horseshoes could be stored about anywhere if they don't get damp and rust."

"Yes, that's right. Don't let your *horseshoes* rust," the banker said, laughing.

Slocum and Elena left. The cold, thin mountain air tore at his lungs and felt wonderful.

"Let's go to the hotel," Elena said. "I am tired from traveling so long."

"This hotel's not like the one in Denver," Slocum pointed out.

"Perhaps we can find one or two things to make it seem . . . similar."

Slocum and Elena did the best they could on a smaller bed with a lumpy mattress and no tub with hot running water.

The next morning it was time to find the scar-faced man.

14

"The counterfeit coins will be in Denver by tomorrow evening," Elena Warburton said, standing back as the train pulled out of the station. Cinders and a spray of mud cascaded down on her as the wheels dug down on the steel rails and the locomotive built up speed.

"Think Pullman can handle them?"

"You don't like Mr. Pullman, do you? Why not? He is quite an effective field agent."

"He treats you like trash."

"I have not said this before, but, well, John, this is my first field mission. Mr. Pullman argued my case most effectively to convince my superiors to give me this opportunity."

Slocum snorted. Elena was more clever and daring than Josiah Pullman could ever be, even in his dreams. Memory of the shoddy disguise Pullman had used to gather information would give Slocum a good chuckle for years to come.

"What do we do now? How do we find this scarred miscreant?"

"That's a question I have yet to answer," Slocum said. "I need to know more about how a counterfeiter works." He took her arm and steered her away from the train depot toward a café. After their prior night's vigorous activities and the effort needed to lug the heavy bags of lead coins to the train station, he had built up quite an appetite.

"I'll tell you what I can." She pursed her lips, then began. "First, the materials required for the planchet are assembled."

"Lead?"

"This is not too difficult to find since so little is necessary, actually. A pound of lead would provide fifteen or twenty coins. The weight is similar enough that most people cannot tell the difference, although pure gold is softer than lead."

"The planchet is more than lead. It has milling."

"Yes, after the lead is poured, the edges are scored to look like a real coin, but it still looks all gray and inert."

"How is that done?"

"Well, I don't exactly know, but if a long semihard cylinder of lead is rolled along a scored sheet, this will place the milling on the edges. Then the metal is hardened and the planchets made by sawing off slugs of the proper thickness."

He and Elena ordered breakfast. Slocum sipped at a cup of coffee but didn't taste the bitter brew because his mind was on the process of counterfeiting. He set down his cup with a click in the saucer.

"What if this operation isn't about just a few coins?"

"A few! Why, John, you almost broke your back carrying the bogus coins this morning. That is not 'a few.' If anything, this is the largest counterfeiting operation to come along in years."

"They are only testing their techniques," Slocum said. "This is a way for them to see if they need to change any part of their scheme."

"I'm not following you."

"Twenty thousand dollars is only the start," Slocum said. "Pretending to rob the train but actually swapping the counterfeit coins for the real ones is how they intend to operate.

Passing coins one at a time, such as the Eakin kid tried with me, is too slow."

"Then why did the Eakins get involved?"

"The ring needed operating money, and that was how they did it. Think of blasting in a mine. You see the huge explosion, but it all started with a match being applied to the end of a fuse."

"So they have to build up their capital to . . . what?"

"A huge counterfeiting operation," Slocum said.

"But this *is* huge!"

"You're thinking small. Whoever is the leader of this gang thinks big. Bigger than big. He is going for millions of dollars in counterfeit coins."

"That's not possible."

"It was only luck that I was there to see the outlaws escape after the train robbery with the actual double eagles. Otherwise, the fakes would have been stored in the bank vault and used as payroll, with none the wiser."

"Somebody would have noticed eventually."

"Eventually," Slocum said, "but not all that soon."

"You've got an idea, John. What is it?" Elena leaned forward, almost upsetting her coffee cup. Her eyes bored into him, but he felt a reluctance to let her know what bothered him. "Tell me."

"For a big operation that can substitute thousands of coins, they need to counterfeit thousands of coins. That would require a lot of lead."

"They could buy it," she said.

"You can ask around town, but I suspect they aren't paying for a wagon load. They're smarter than that since people might ask questions."

"They can get the lead anywhere. It doesn't have to be here, even if the town's name is Leadville. More than lead comes out of these mines. Lots more."

"All the more reason to make the bogus coins here. So much money flows in and out of this town that substituting some of it will finance their operation for months. And they don't have to pass the coins here. They can make them, ship them back to Denver, and spread out through the West."

Elena sat a little straighter.

"Or ship them back East, where people aren't as suspicious about counterfeits. Whoever in their right mind would bite down on a gold coin in New York or Chicago to see if it was a fake?"

"Might be folks are more suspicious out here." What Elena said cemented his notion that the counterfeiters had done all they could to prove that the scheme worked. Train robberies that were "thwarted" could cover the substitution of the coins made here in Leadville—or nearby.

"Where do we start?" Elena asked.

Slocum leaned back as the waiter delivered their food. He inhaled deeply, and his belly rumbled. It had been a spell since he had eaten.

"We start with the eggs," he said.

"I haven't found any purchase of lead that is unusual," Elena said, dejected.

"The town smithy—the marshal called him Leon—is the only place I haven't checked," Slocum said. "You been asking about gold?"

"It wouldn't do any good," she said. "The counterfeiters can get the gold anywhere, even melt down a couple real coins since all they need is a very thin sheet. A single gold coin can be flattened into a sheet a couple yards square. Put the thin sheet over the planchet, heat it a mite, and the fake is completed."

"So it's the lead we look for." He laughed without humor. There were dozens of abandoned mines all around the mountains surrounding Leadville. All the counterfeiters needed was one played-out mine, but with enough left in a vein for their purposes, to get what they needed.

"The stamping equipment might be another possible source of information."

"You mean to see if the station agent remembers it being brought in from Denver?"

"Can't hurt," she said. She looked around, didn't see anyone looking in their direction, and gave him a quick kiss on the lips. "That didn't hurt either."

She went off, making sure to sway her behind to give him a hint of what waited for him that night when they had finished a long day of asking questions and not getting answers. Only Slocum wanted there to be a tad of victory to their night. A celebration if he found out where the counterfeiters were holed up would be more fun than a consolation roll in the hay.

He set out for the blacksmith's shop at the edge of town. The smell of burning iron wrinkled his nose before he got close enough to hear the rhythmic clang of the hammer hitting hot metal. Through the open door, Leon lifted his hammer and smashed it expertly into a horseshoe bent over his anvil. He was stripped to the waist and sweating from the heat boiling out of his forge. Slocum knew at a glance he didn't want to tangle with the man, at least not with bare knuckles. Leon was powerful enough to rip the leg off a horse if it struck him as something worth doing.

The smith looked up as Slocum stood in the doorway.

"Help you, mister?" The blacksmith didn't pause in his work.

"I need to buy a couple pounds of lead. Can you help me out?"

"Couple pounds? You lookin' to start a war?"

"Don't want it for bullets," Slocum said.

"Then what? Heard tell a lead sinker on a fishin' line works wonders, but I prefer to use a trout fly." A loud hiss like a steam engine venting from its pistons sounded as he thrust his horseshoe into a quenching tub of water. Leon held up his work, eyed it critically, then tossed it into a box filled with sand.

"If you can't sell me enough, who could?"

"Mister, there are a dozen mines around in these here mountains. Any of them would be happy to hand you the ore and let you pick it out with your teeth."

"Who needs the money the most?"

Leon laughed as he began pumping the bellows to renew the coals. In a few seconds they glowed with an eye-dazzling orange. He kept at it until they were the proper color, and then he shoved an iron bar among them.

"Who doesn't? Ain't a single rock monkey out there what don't need money."

"I want to be helpful. You got a friend in such a position?"

Leon looked up and squinted.

"I seen you before? You look familiar."

"I've been around town for a while. Came in from Denver." Slocum wondered if Leon was shortsighted from the way he squinted. If so, it made it less likely he'd identify Slocum as the man with Marshal Atkinson inquiring after the use of his forge and equipment a few nights earlier.

"Don't get out much. The missus keeps me roped up and near the kennel, if you know what I mean."

"Friends?"

"Well, there's a miner down on his luck at the Sorry Times Mine. His name for that pit says it all. Name's Sookie Clark."

Slocum stood a little straighter. This was the man Leon had blamed for ruining the temper of his hammer.

"Where might I find him?"

"In his mine, if he's got any sense. He owes me money for bustin' up my—" Leon stopped and squinted harder at Slocum. "I seen you before?"

"Thanks," Slocum said, hastily leaving. He wasn't sure how nearsighted Leon might be, but it wouldn't do if he got a bee in his bonnet and asked questions Slocum wasn't inclined to answer.

Slocum went to the livery and dickered with the owner over the bill owed for stabling his mare. They finally came to an agreement and Slocum asked, "Where might I find the Sorry Times?"

"Five miles along the road leadin' south outta town," the stableman said. "If you got business with that Sookie Clark, you tell him he still owes me eight dollars for takin' care of his swayback mule whilst he was in Denver gallivantin' about."

"I'll do that," Slocum said, saddling and leading his horse from the stables. He stepped up and rode out of Leadville at a brisk trot. Why would a down-on-his-luck miner like Sookie Clark need to go to Denver, even for a day or two? And if he did, why come back to a worthless mine? Unless he had new business partners.

The spring day turned chilly with the promise of rain hanging in the air, but Slocum pushed on. He might have to spend the night on the trail but thought Elena would understand, especially if he located the counterfeiters' source of lead.

Alert as he was, he almost missed the road to the Sorry Times. A signpost had once held crosspieces with a dozen names on it but had fallen into a ditch, where water and wind had rotted the wood and faded the names into oblivion. Only by using his imagination did Slocum make out the name SORRY TIMES MINE on the bottommost sign. The road was overgrown with weeds, and nothing heavier than a buggy could have gone up the winding road into the hills within the past few weeks. Even considering the heavy rain would wash away the tracks, the road was virtually untrammeled. The vegetation alongside the trail and the way the weeds popped up told him that much.

But a hint here and there of a horse recently going uphill but not returning showed plain enough to his expert eye.

Slocum rode almost a mile into a canyon. Deserted mines vomited out their tailings from their mouths to dribble down the steep slopes. Nowhere did he see men occupied in the mines or hear the telltale clank of machines working any of the claims. The entire canyon had petered out sometime back.

From what Leon and the stableman had told him, Sookie Clark was like any of those mines—all petered out.

The sound of a braying mule alerted him he was getting close. Slocum led his mare into a ravine, studied the sky to guess how long before a storm might fill it bank to bank with water, then decided he had plenty of time. He patted the horse's neck, looped the reins around a juniper branch, and began climbing.

He went straight up the side of the canyon until he reached a road blasted into the rock. It led to a mine with a white-washed sign proclaiming it to be the LUCKY BASTARD MINE. Part of the name might have been accurate. Slocum kicked through the dross at the mine's mouth and saw nothing that looked like blue dirt or anything of value. A man had wasted his time here before moving on.

Slocum hiked around to the side of the mine and saw the mule making all the noise not thirty yards distant. To reach the animal, he would have to climb down the hillside he was on, then claw his way up a steep incline of twenty feet or so. In the shadows he made out a dark opening into that hill.

And coming from it was a smallish man with pipe stem arms. He had a rope over his shoulder, bent forward and digging in his toes to pull like a beast of burden. Inch by inch he gained and an ore cart finally came into view. Slocum hunkered down and watched, wondering why Sookie Clark—if this was the man he sought—didn't hitch the mule to the cart and save himself some effort.

It came to him that the mule might be smarter than the man.

The man he took to be Clark stopped pulling and began

rummaging through the rusty ore cart, tossing out rocks as big as his head onto a sheet of canvas. When he'd emptied his load, he began moving them downhill by dragging the canvas. Once the miner was out of sight, Slocum scooted and slipped and slid downhill to where the mule stood patiently. It turned a big brown eye in his direction but didn't let out any protest at all seeing a newcomer to the claim.

Slocum found climbing the steep hill to the mine a chore, but he came to the brink near the edge of the mine and peered over it. Clark was hard at work loading his ore into a crusher. Beyond, Slocum saw a kiln, but it wasn't fired up. The man needed a significant load of crushed ore before working to reduce the lead and discard the dross.

Grunting, Slocum pulled himself over the edge and rolled through the dust to crouch behind the ore cart. If Clark would scrape off the rust and oil the wheels, his job would be far easier. Somehow, Slocum doubted that extra bit of work had ever occurred to the miner.

He half rose, considering his chances of learning anything by confronting Clark.

Looking around, he saw a sign that had once been nailed to a wooden mine support lying on the ground. He could barely make out the lettering but got enough of SORRY TIMES to know this *was* the man he sought. The way he ground up the ore so lackadaisically convinced Slocum that Leon wasn't wrong. Sookie Clark was the sort who would misuse another's tools, and never know the reason.

"You got more lead for me?" came the call from downhill. Slocum strained to see who greeted Clark but couldn't get a good look. He heard the steady clopping of a horse working up a road he had missed.

"Not yet, Mr. Bulwer, not jist yet. Been hard scratchin' out the ore. Not much left in the old Sorry Times."

"I'm ready to mill again, and all I have is fifty pounds. I need at least that much more."

Slocum involuntarily stood and stared. A hundred pounds

of fake coins? He quickly ran through the possibilities. This Bulwer was ready to counterfeit another thirty-five thousand dollars' worth of coins!

Slocum reached for his six-shooter, prepared to end the counterfeiting ring here and now. Letting Clark go was easy enough. The man was more of a danger to himself than anyone else, but if Bulwer was the ringleader, then Slocum could count on a huge reward from the Pinkerton Detective Agency. And he knew how he would spend it. A room in the Brown Palace back in Denver, with a soft bed and running bathwater—and Elena Warburton.

"Gosh, Mr. Bulwer, that's danged near two hundred pounds of lead you've already got from me."

"I'll take as much as you can mine, but you're not working fast enough." The man rode into view. Slocum caught his breath, and lifted his six-gun. The rider—Bulwer—was the man with the scar running across his nose.

He started to shout out for Bulwer to grab some sky when the sound of more horses froze him. Three more men rode up. There wasn't any way Slocum could take all four of them prisoner.

"Boss, we found a horse down in a ravine."

"You got more than the mule, Clark?"

"No, sir, I don't. Can't hardly afford the mule, what with the medicine I got to give her and—"

"You don't have a horse, too?"

"Nope."

"Fan out. There's somebody around here snooping on us," Bulwer said, reaching for his own pistol.

Slocum tucked his six-shooter back into his holster and looked back down the hill. He caught his breath when he saw another of the counterfeiters standing guard over his horse. If he tried to drop down that sheer cliff, he would be seen for sure.

Bulwer's three gunmen dismounted and started up the hill, coming straight for Slocum.

15

Slocum wasn't sure if they had spotted him. He hid behind the rusty ore cart for a moment, looked over the brink of the twenty-foot drop to where Clark's mule stood patiently, thinking its mulish thoughts and not giving a damn about the hubbub around it. Slocum duckwalked into the mine and stood just inside the mouth, heart hammering away as he heard the boot steps crunching on gravel and getting nearer by the second. He drew his six-shooter, but he didn't have any better chance now of shooting his way out of this predicament than he did before. Less. He was backed into the mine now. He cursed himself for being so stupid. Better to die out in the open than in a ready-made grave.

"I heard something, boss," shouted one gunman. The footsteps stopped. Slocum imagined the trio pulling their iron and looking around for something to shoot.

He slipped deeper into the mine. Ten steps inside, the mine branched. Each direction along the fork was equally dark. He went right for no good reason. With his luck running the way it had, he was as likely to die in this stope as he was in the other. Slocum turned and waited when the darkness engulfed him completely. The faint glow from outside would silhouette anyone coming down the shaft, giving him the opportunity to eliminate one of his opponents. He doubted Bulwer had brought more than four henchmen with him, but such a guess could leave him dead.

Just like picking the wrong shaft to follow.

"You see anything?" Bulwer shouted.

"Nothing, boss. I got a look down to where Sookie's staked his mule, but nobody's movin' 'tween there and where Johnny's found the horse."

"Might be," piped up Clark, "somebody snuck into the mine. They might want to steal my lead."

"Shut up," Bulwer said. "Nobody would steal the pathetic ore you pull from that mine. Hell, I don't know why I pay you top dollar for it."

Slocum knew. If Sookie Clark worked hard and got just enough to keep him going, he wasn't likely to go into Leadville and tell anyone he was making money from a played-out mine. Such a statement would brand him as a liar or crazy, which would make him prove his contention. The last thing in the world Bulwer wanted was for a bunch of half-drunk miners to troop out here to see that Clark had been working the mine and had pulled a fair amount of lead from it.

He ran his hand over the mine wall, tracing out the lead carbonate that sometimes carried silver along with it. The precious metal was missing, but the low-grade lead ore was more valuable to Bulwer and the counterfeiters than silver would be. They could turn a pound of lead into a pound of gold. To actually mine silver for that kind of value, they'd have to dig out tons of ore, maybe hundreds of tons.

"What do you want us to do, boss?"

"Get your asses into the mine and see if Clark's right about someone snooping in there. If you see him, kill him."

Slocum clutched his pistol a little tighter. His life had come down to this moment. He wanted to take as many of the counterfeiting ring with him as he could before they gunned him down.

"We'd be sittin' ducks bullin' our way in," the gunman said uneasily.

"Send Sookie in first. Let him flush out your fox."

Slocum saw shadows moving at the mouth of the mine and Clark protesting. Then a figure stumbled in. Pressing himself against the wall, he waited as Clark came to the fork. If the miner went down the other way, he had a respite. He might walk out boldly, the gunmen thinking he was Clark. That could give a few seconds' advantage.

Sookie Clark walked straight toward Slocum.

"I don't want to shoot you, but I will if you let on you've found me," Slocum said.

"Y-You ain't s'pposed to be in here. This is a workin' mine."

"Tell me how to leave without getting ventilated, and you'll never see me again."

"Back that way," Clark began. He swallowed his words in a gulp that sounded as if he was choking. "They'd shoot you for certain sure."

Slocum said nothing.

"You finding anything in there, Sookie? You need help?"

"Answer them," Slocum said in a low voice. He lifted his Colt Navy so the miner could see it in his rock-steady hand.

"Not findin' nothin' yet."

"Keep going!"

"Yes, sir, Mr. Bulwer. I'll do that."

"Where does this shaft lead? A dead end?"

"Not exactly," Clark said. "I cut a drain hole in the back of this branch. Was gettin' knee-deep water, so—"

"I get the picture," Slocum said. "Is it big enough for a man to squeeze through?"

"Hell, I lost my good ore cart down it. It's mighty big and took danged near a case of dynamite to blast."

Slocum started backing up. He motioned for Clark to remain between him and mouth of the mine.

"How far back?"

"We're danged near there, mister. But you can't git out that way."

"You said it was big enough to swallow up an ore cart."

"That's the problem. The ore cart's stuck down the drain. Water gets around it, but you'd never fit."

"Who's Bulwer?"

"What's that?" Clark was confused by the sudden change in Slocum's questions.

"He have his hideout somewhere nearby?" That was what Slocum would do if he were the counterfeiter. Why haul the lead very far? When they were finished with Sookie Clark, they'd kill him, maybe stuff his body in the mine and collapse it. Or if they wanted to be even more clever, they could make it look like an accident. Mining was dangerous, and from the condition of Sookie's equipment, nobody would question that he had brought on his death himself through poor maintenance.

"I don't know 'bout no hideout, but Mr. Bulwer's got a fancy metal working rig set up in the next canyon over. Sometimes at night, I hear him poundin' away to beat the band. Don't know what he's makin' but it takes a powerful lot of my lead—and he pays top dollar for it. See?"

Slocum tensed when the miner reached for a vest pocket. But Clark only pulled out a coin and held it up. In the dim light Slocum saw the faint golden reflection. If Clark had bothered to check the coin, he would have found that Bulwer had given him back some of the lead he mined in the form of a fake double eagle.

"A generous man," Slocum said, not trying to hide his sarcasm. Clark missed the tone entirely.

"Yes, sir, he is. But he kin git mighty testy if I don't work the mine hard enough. I ought to be down there crushin' my ore and smeltin' out the lead from the carbonate right this minute."

"Show me the drain first."

"Not more 'n fifty feet deeper. I quit this shaft 'cuz the vein of ore petered out on me and left nothing but worthless rock."

Slocum quickly covered half that distance, then backed up more carefully, a foot feeling the floor as he went in case Clark's memory wasn't so good or the miner was trying to do the work of the three outlaws outside for them.

His boot slipped on damp stone that slid downward sharply.

"This is it. See? I marked the wall with a cut. Real deep cut and put an arrow on it so I'd know where it was, even in the dark. I work a lot in the dark since I can't always afford miner's candles."

Slocum chanced spinning around and kneeling to probe the drain. His hand rammed hard into metal only inches down. The ore cart. Tracing the outline in the dark gave him a touch of hope. The cart had fallen in and wedged at an angle.

"This cart as big as the one you're still using?"

"Reckon so. Never had call to measure them."

"Does it load as much ore?" Slocum asked, putting it into terms Clark could better understand.

"Surely does. Might even hold twenty-thirty pounds more."

"The drain goes outside?"

"Out of the hillside down into the ravine next to where I keep my mule."

"Go back and tell Bulwer that you didn't find anybody here. He'll be real mad at you if you tell him you found anyone and let him get away."

"But he asked me to find you. Well, not him but his partners."

"Same thing. Bulwer will be mad. You don't want that. It's a white lie to make him feel good."

"I don't like to hurt nobody's feelin's," Clark admitted.

"Go on back and tell them nobody's here."

"Well, if you say so . . ."

Clark hesitated, then retraced the path from the mine. Slocum tucked away his six-shooter and slid the leather thong over the hammer to keep from losing it. He pictured how the cart had fallen into the drain and knew he had to be agile but could get through if he forced himself into the hopper and found the lower portion sticking out just enough to give him space to squeeze through.

He went headfirst into the hopper, twisted around the bottom, and squeezed past on the lower part of the cart. Slocum scraped off clothes and skin but got around the cart. Getting his legs and feet clear took a bit more work than he expected. He finally grabbed a slippery rock and pulled as hard as he could to get free. When he did, he slid down the drain like it was spitting out a watermelon seed. One instant he was surrounded by slime-slick rock and the next he was tumbling through the air. He landed hard enough to momentarily stun him not ten feet from the mule.

The critter turned one big brown eye on him with a "You again?" look.

Slocum got his wits about him, then found he could hardly stand because of the pain in his side. The stab wound Elena had inflicted was healing well but had again opened up during his precipitous exit from the mine. Clutching his side, he forced away the pain and stumbled a few more steps before flopping down behind a rotting log. The wood was soaked through and through because it was directly under the drain from the mine.

"You see anything, Johnny?" Bulwer shouted.

Slocum hunkered down as the man guarding his horse called back, "Don't see anything. You want me to bring the horse on up to you?"

"We'll keep looking, for a while longer." Bulwer disappeared from the edge of the cliff, but Slocum heard him talking to Clark. Although he caught only every few words, Slocum knew that Clark had figured out his own life hung in the balance and denied seeing anyone in the mine.

"Get in there and flush out the varmint. All three of you!"

Slocum knew he had to make a bid for freedom now or he would be pinned down. It was getting toward twilight, and with all three of Bulwer's gunmen inside the mine, that meant fewer eyes to spot him. If Clark kept his tater trap shut, Slocum might make it back to his mare.

The mule looked at him, shook its head, and brayed before going back to cropping at the sparse grass in front of it.

Even the mule mocked him.

Wincing, Slocum got to his feet, judged distances, and began walking. His first steps were tentative, then he convinced himself he dared not be in the open overlong or Bulwer might spot him. He reached the base of the hill where he had slid down. All he had to do was get up the hill, down into the ravine, and ride away.

Get down into the ravine and eliminate Bulwer's henchman still guarding his horse, he amended.

The pain turned to a dull ache, but he felt the wound oozing blood as he dug his toes into the rocky slope and started climbing. The twilight kept him from being an obvious target from over at the Sorry Times Mine, but the best he could hope for was everyone's attention being focused inside the mine.

He reached the top of the slope and looked down into the ravine. He saw his mare waiting patiently for him, but the guard was nowhere to be seen. Slocum edged down, favoring his side. As he got closer to his horse, he heard a hissing noise and knew the guard was to his right taking a leak against a tree trunk. Slocum reached for his six-shooter but immediately discovered that he couldn't grip the ebony handle because his right side had turned slick with his own blood.

Moving slowly, listening to the man's satisfied sigh as he finished, Slocum knew he had to risk everything or get caught the instant the man turned from the tree. He caught up a fist-sized rock that was rough enough not to slip and ran forward.

Bulwer's gunman heard the noise but was too slow to identify the danger. Slocum brought the rock up and down in a powerful swing. Even so, the rock slid from his grip as he smashed it into the man's head. The slick blood hampering his hold and the man's Stetson robbed the blow of the power Slocum had intended. He wouldn't have been displeased if he had crushed the man's skull. As it was, the blow drove the gunman to his knees and wrenched a moan from his lips.

Slocum kicked as hard as he could, caught the man on the point of his chin, and then lost his balance, crashing backward. He landed hard enough to stun himself again. Pain filled his world, and the blackness creeping in all around threatened to permanently engulf him. Slocum fought the tide washing over him and sat up. His opponent lay still on the ground.

Rolling to hands and knees, Slocum painfully stood and staggered to his horse. Getting into the saddle was a chore, but Slocum kept thinking what Bulwer would do to him if he got caught. And then there was Elena. He wanted to feel Elena's fingers stroking over his forehead, lacing through his hair. He wanted her warm, sensuous body next to his.

He turned his horse and headed back to the road leading to Leadville. He fought off unconsciousness for several miles and then the pain possessed him totally. He wobbled in the saddle and guided his horse off the road to give himself a chance to recover.

John Slocum slid from the saddle and crashed to the ground, his world entirely black.

16

"John, wake up."

Slocum moaned and tried to roll onto his side. Too much pain. He curled up in a tight ball.

"Come on, you're too heavy for me to lift. John!"

It was a good dream, but the details were blurred with pain. He groaned as he felt himself being pressed flat on the ground and heard cloth ripping.

"Oh my God!"

"Nice to have you in my dream," he murmured. Then he cried out as pain stabbed into his side. He tried to turn away, but weight held him flat. More cloth tore and then came feathery light touches on his belly. He forced his eyes open and instantly closed them. The sunlight almost blinded him. Nothing made any sense.

"There, that ought to help. Can you stand? Are you even awake?"

"Elena?"

"Who else?"

Squinting, he saw that the woman straddled his waist but not as delightfully as she had when she was naked and in the bathtub. She had torn strips from her skirt and had bound his wound—the stab wound she had inflicted on him. She got off him and grabbed his wrists, pulling him upright. He almost passed out as pain thrust through his side like a brand-new knife wound.

Then he was on his feet, her arm around him and walking him toward his horse.

"Didn't wander off last night," he said.

"Didn't wander off two days ago," Elena said. "I've been frantic. I thought you—"

"You thought I'd run out on you?" He had to laugh and instantly regretted it. Clutching his side, he kept moving to his horse and gingerly stepped up. "Wouldn't do that. Not when I found out the counterfeiter's name."

"There's time for that later. I have to get you to the town doctor."

"No sawbones. They kill more than they heal. Just let me sleep some."

"Very well, but only if you don't pass out before we get to the hotel. I'll be watching."

"Two days?" Slocum hardly believed he had lain in the dirt so long, snuffed out like a candle flame.

"I talked with Leon and got directions to the Sorry Times and just happened to see your horse."

"Best horse I've ever had," Slocum said, leaning forward to pat the horse's neck. He almost tumbled from the saddle. Catching himself, he gripped the pommel with both hands and held on. His brain wasn't working right. How could he have his hands on the pommel? Where were the reins? He saw them swinging out and up into Elena's grip. She was leading him back to town.

That was all right. All right.

Slocum woke up with a start.

"It's about time. You've slept close to ten hours."

"Since you found me?" He looked to the hotel room window. The flickering gas light outside and the distant roar of drunken miners overflowing the saloons told him it was night again.

"You were delirious but said you had found out who the ringleader is."

"Bulwer," he said, trying out the name. His tongue felt three times too big for his mouth and cotton wool had been stuffed into every crevice. He sipped at water Elena held for him. He felt better. "His men called him Bulwer."

"Anton Bulwer," she said. "I know of him, but he doesn't have a scar on his face. Is the man you call Bulwer the one with the scar?"

Slocum nodded. He tried to sort through all the conflicting images in his brain. His side didn't pain him as much. He belched and tasted whiskey. Then he saw the half-empty bottle on the nightstand. Elena had been giving him the best kind of painkiller.

"Who is he?"

"He used to work for the Department of the Treasury as an engraver. He worked with paper money, making the plates used to print scrip, but he was versatile. He was fired because of a discrepancy in the amount of paper he bought and the number of bills he printed. Bulwer claimed there was wastage, but he couldn't prove it because the trash was examined and only a few misprinted bills were discovered. They thought he might have stolen thousands of dollars in real money."

"Money he printed?"

"It's difficult to find the printing press, paper, and ink for a decent counterfeiting of paper money. But he's skilled. He was the best engraver the Treasury ever hired, but after he was fired, he just disappeared."

"How do you know of him?"

"Pinkerton was hired to locate him and try to recover the money he had stolen. His name and description were sent to all the offices, but no one ever spotted him."

"The scar might be a burn," Slocum said. "I've never gotten a good look but could it come from hot metal spattering his face?"

"Learning to forge metal can be dangerous, especially if you're teaching yourself. There are manuals describing how to etch a stamp and the rest of the minting process. A mistake could have scarred him."

"Is there a reward for him?"

"There was never proof he had actually stolen the printed money, so he was never formally charged." Elena shook her head. "He was wanted so we could trail him and find the money. That would be proof of a crime, we could arrest him and . . . well, there might have been a reward then. More likely, Mr. Pinkerton would have turned him over to the government in exchange for goodwill."

"But if he is actually counterfeiting coins?"

"The government would certainly offer a reward for that." Elena made a face, and Slocum remembered her displeasure with him before when it seemed that he sought only a reward. At the moment, he didn't much care. He owed her for saving him—probably saving his life. But he wouldn't have been in the situation if she hadn't stabbed him.

"The mine owner said he'd already sold Bulwer a couple hundred pounds of lead."

"A couple *hundred*?" Elena stared at him in disbelief. "That would mean he . . ."

"He's likely on his way to making hundreds of thousands of dollars' worth of counterfeit coins."

"Oh, my," she said in a weak voice. She took a drink of the water she still held, then said, "I must contact Mr. Pullman with this information. He'll know what to do."

"Don't you?"

"What do you mean?"

"You're a Pinkerton detective. This Anton Bulwer is wanted by your agency and is likely responsible for robbing a train and making more pinchbeck coins than either of us could count. Why wait for Pullman to tell you to do what you know has to be done?" Slocum didn't want the other detective getting in the way. If Pullman came to Leadville, he would only make capturing Bulwer more difficult.

Slocum felt he had a score to settle, if not a reward to earn.

"I should let him know so he can contact the home office," Elena said, wrestling with duty versus common sense. Common sense won out. "What do we do to find Bulwer?"

"He's moving heavy loads of lead. He must be shipping out the fake coins some way since keeping them here won't do him any good."

"Do you think he knows that he lost the gold coins from the robbery?"

"Would Timmins admit it to his boss?" Slocum thought on this a moment and finally said, "I doubt he did. Whatever Timmins was supposed to do with the stolen gold isn't going to happen now. Timmins won't fess up since, from what I saw of Bulwer, he's likely to have him killed."

"So Bulwer is still moving his fake coins, thinking his plan is working to perfection."

Slocum nodded. That was the way he saw it. The market for counterfeit coins in Leadville was saturated, and if too many miners caught on to receiving phony pay, they would burn the town to the ground. Bulwer would be forced to find another place for his production. Since the banker was issuing real coins again, no hue and cry would go up and Bulwer had no reason to believe his plans weren't still good.

"How many independent freighters are there in town?"

"Only a handful. The mines would use their own equipment and drivers."

"It doesn't look as if Bulwer is moving his fakes to Denver on the train. That leaves only wagons or pack animals."

"In these mountains, pack mules might be useful, but where is he sending the coins?"

"That," Slocum said, "is what we have to find out. Try to

ask around without stirring up too much dust. Bulwer thinks he's cock of the walk right now, and we shouldn't do anything to disturb that arrogance."

"Are you going to be all right, John? You look so pale."

He swung his legs over the side of the bed. While weak, he wasn't dizzy. Flexing his hand and moving his arm around gave him some twinges in his side, but not enough to get in the way if he had to use his six-gun. The trouble before had been too much blood turning his hand slippery. He might not be able to whip his weight in wildcats but his hand was steady and strong enough to shoot them.

With a surge, he stood beside the bed and moved around.

"You're sure, John?"

"Time's a'wasting," he said. He began dressing.

"I'm sorry about your shirt and vest. There wasn't time for me to have the blood cleaned off."

Slocum settled them around his body and noted how stiff they were. Putting on his coat and buttoning it hid most of the blood so he wouldn't have to answer unwanted questions. When he strapped on his gun belt, he winced. The weight on his hip forced him to tilt enough to put a strain on his wound.

"You don't look good," she said.

"But you do. You look better than good. You look fine." Slocum pulled her to him and kissed her. For a moment, she resisted, then melted.

When they broke off, Elena said, "You'd better be just fine. You'd better be!"

Slocum laughed, settled his hat on his head, held out his arm for Elena, and together they left the hotel. In the street, they split up, Elena going to check a freight company at the northern end of town while he went south. He found a small office attached to a stable and went inside. The teamster behind a desk looked up and gave Slocum a broken-toothed smile.

"If you're bringin' me business, you're my favorite customer."

"Not so much freight to haul?" Slocum guessed.

"Been mighty slim pickin's for the entire winter. Spring usually sees a pickup in business but not so far this year. So, I can make you a fine deal. What do you have to move?"

From what the freighter said, Slocum knew he had to look elsewhere.

"How's your competition doing?"

"Rafe? Same as me until a week back. Won't tell me who he's workin' for since he knows I'd undercut his rates."

"You ought to pick up the local dray work since Rafe's doing the long hauls."

"You'd think," the man said. "He's got his biggest wagon—the biggest that'll fit the mountain roads, at least—heading south to Alamosa or maybe Pueblo. Can't imagine what freight he'd bring back."

"Maybe the one-way trip is profitable enough?"

"Could be," the freighter said. "Can't imagine what that is. Now, how big's the cargo you want me to move for you?"

"Since you're available, I'll report that back to my boss," Slocum said, leaving as graciously as he could since he had learned what he needed.

He hurried the length of Leadville to find the other freight company, the one a man named Rafe operated. Slocum had hardly stepped out into the main street when he heard horses protesting loudly and a wagon's traces creaking with strain. The wagon rolled past, the driver snapping his blacksnake whip above the ears of the lead horses.

"Giddy-yap, you fugitives from a glue factory," the driver shouted.

"Rafe! Wait up!" Slocum waved his arms. He drew the driver's attention. The man's eyes went wide in surprise—or was it fear? He cracked his whip again to race past Slocum.

Two steps, then three, and Slocum grabbed hold of the endgate. He pulled himself up and looked into the wagon bed. All that was there were piles of blankets mounded up and tied securely. Rafe was in a powerful hurry to get somewhere so he could pick up his cargo.

"Where are you heading? I want to hire you!"

The driver half turned and swung his whip around. There wasn't any force in it, but the crack caught Slocum around the upper thigh. The impact smarted but wasn't as bad as the throbbing wound in his side. However, the impact unbalanced him and caused him to tumble back into the street, where he landed in mud. A few townspeople on the boardwalks laughed and then hastily looked away when he glared at them.

Slocum climbed to his feet and watched Rafe rattle out of town. He considered getting his horse and chasing down the freighter, then realized what the sudden, panicked departure meant. Rafe was on his way to pick up a shipment from Anton Bulwer. Following him would lead to the counterfeiter—but Rafe was panicky. That meant only one thing.

Wiping off the mud the best he could as he walked, Slocum saw only a single bright spot about such filth all over him. It hid the way his shirt and vest were bloodstained. When he'd finished with his clothing, he drew his six-shooter and used his shirttail to wipe off the mud that threatened to foul the firing mechanism.

Rafe hightailing it from town meant that Elena had spooked him by asking uncomfortable questions.

Slocum cocked his gun, then stopped in front of the freight company door. It stood partially open. With a quick kick, Slocum knocked it back against the wall so hard that glass shattered. He ignored the tinkle of broken glass as he spun into the room.

Empty.

Slocum saw something on the floor, partially hidden by

an overturned chair. He pounced on it and held up Elena's purse. Her small six-shooter was still inside. Slocum stormed out the back door in time to see two riders bringing their horses from the corral.

"Hold on!"

One man went for his pistol. Slocum fired twice, then a third time and brought the man down. The wounded man used both hands to lift his six-gun and got off a shot that went high. He fought to fire again, but it wasn't in him. The pistol slipped from his fingers as he fell facedown into the mud.

The other man swung into the saddle, put his heels to the horse's flanks, and shot off like a skyrocket, bent low and hugging his horse's neck. Slocum rushed out to get a better shot, emptied his pistol at the fleeing man, missing with each of the three rounds. The rider skidded in the slippery mud, got around the corner onto a back street, and vanished from sight.

Slocum cursed his bad luck letting the man escape to let Bulwer know somebody else was on his trail. As he went to the man he had plugged, he reloaded.

Slocum stood over the wounded man. He pushed him over with the toe of his boot and pointed his six-shooter directly between his eyes. The man showed no fear.

"I'm a dead man. You don't scare me none."

"Where is she?"

The answer Slocum got was a gurgling cough followed by blood vomiting out the man's mouth and nose.

"She's not gonna be a problem much longer," the outlaw said, gurgling deep in his throat. Then he died.

17

Slocum searched the dead man's pockets and found a half-dozen double eagles. He ran his finger across the milling on one, trying to determine if it was a fake or real. He couldn't tell so he stuck them all into his pocket, then lit out for the stable to fetch his horse. Elena had given good instructions to the stableman on tending the horse. The mare stood well fed, groomed, and ready to ride. Getting into the saddle was harder for Slocum than convincing the horse to once more get on the road.

He turned south. He didn't know where the rider at the freight station had gone, but he did know Rafe's route. There was only the main road big enough for the wagon he drove. Slocum rubbed his thigh where the teamster had used the blacksnake whip to dislodge him from the rear of the wagon. No matter how frightened Rafe might have been, or what innocent role he might play in the counterfeiting ring, Slocum vowed to make the man pay for whipping him.

The traffic along the road was greater than Slocum would have liked, but more than once he called out to a miner either on foot or riding a decrepit horse asking if he had seen Rafe. The answers were always the same. Slocum was on the right trail.

Whether Elena had been in the back of wagon, trussed up under the blankets and gagged, or had been taken by other men at the freight office who had ridden out with her before Slocum arrived, didn't matter. If they hadn't killed her outright, they were taking her to Anton Bulwer. Wherever the master engraver and counterfeiter was holed up was likely to be where he made the phony coins. Slocum could kill two birds with one stone—free Elena and capture Bulwer and his equipment.

He rode until he felt light-headed, then slowed the pace and took a gander at the road. Far past the Sorry Times Mine, he had reached a point where the road began winding down from the elevation into a valley. At first he thought it might be the same one where he had shot it out with several of Bulwer's gang, then decided it cut off in a different direction. This valley was spiderwebbed with small streams and grassy meadows dotted with stands of pine and aspen.

Slocum blinked a couple times to be sure his vision was clear when he thought he spotted a wagon lurching along much lower down the road. Leaning precariously over the verge, he saw fresh tracks on the road not thirty feet under him. Quickly tracing the road brought him to the valley floor, where the wagon finally picked up speed and raced along. At this distance Slocum couldn't tell if Rafe was driving, but how many freighters would come this way?

Deeper in the valley he saw thin tendrils of black smoke rising. Reaching back, he pulled out his spyglass and tried to make out the source of the smoke. It was obscured by the trees and mist in the distance.

Staying on the road didn't seem to afford him much benefit. He had no evidence that Rafe had anything to do with the counterfeiters, though he was willing to bet money— all the coins in his pocket, both real and counterfeit—that he did.

He started down the road, hitting one switchback after another. Slocum looked for a hint as to how heavily laden the wagon was and finally decided it had to be close to empty to leave the depth of tracks it did. A wagon full of material, no matter if it was lead or sacks of flour, would cut deeper ruts.

By the time he reached the valley, he swayed in the saddle and the wagon was long out of sight. He almost laughed as he looked at the grassy terrain. A blind man could follow that track. Slocum dismounted and measured the depth of the ruts and knew that Rafe came to pick up a load, not deliver it. Looking back up the steep road told him the teamster needed some powerful horses for even a moderate load. Going back up the road would kill even a six-horse team if a wagon creaked under the weight of more than a few hundred pounds.

Slocum whistled tunelessly through his teeth, thinking what the value of even a hundred pounds of counterfeit coins would be.

"Elena, are you here?" he said softly. Slocum mounted and began riding, aware that he would be spotted quickly if he approached the source of the smoke in daylight. When he found a draw, he rode down into it and let his horse graze on the fresh spring grass while he stretched out in the afternoon sun. It was warm on his face and he hurt. How he hurt!

He came awake with a start when he realized it was well past sundown. Along the floor of the valley, sunset came fast and early, but a quick study of the stars convinced him that he had slept—passed out—for more than six hours. Getting some jerky from his saddlebags, he gnawed it and then had to sate his thirst by hiking a few yards to a clear-running stream. The cold water, both swallowed and dashed on his face, perked him up more than a few cups of coffee would have.

He mounted and continued the ride toward the curlicues of smoke, now visible in the night as a sliver of moonlight turned them into dancing liquid silver. If Bulwer felt secure here, he wouldn't post guards, but Slocum doubted the counterfeiter would ever rest. The man had a devious mind to come up with the scheme for substituting his bogus coins for real ones in "botched" robberies. Not only had he swapped the fake for the real, but the law wasn't as inclined to come after an inept robber. A marshal could belly up to the bar and tell stories of stupid robbers and garner drinks from half those in the saloon.

The perfect crime was one that no one believed to have happened.

As Slocum neared a stand of junipers mixed with cottonwoods along a stream, he heard the steady whap-whap of heavy machinery. Dismounting, he approached on foot to scout the buildings. A forge glowed dull orange in the night, and two men worked to hold something with tongs while another swung a small hammer. A fourth man circled like a vulture, pointing, directing, giving new instructions. Slocum had found Anton Bulwer hard at work supervising his men in the fine art of counterfeiting coins.

Away from the forge was a low shed. Parked some distance away Slocum saw the wagon and ten horses, maybe more, in a large corral. A man circled the corral, but he watched the horses rather than out into the darkness.

Slocum circled to come up on the corral to get a better look at the man.

"Goldangit," the man muttered to himself, unaware Slocum was close enough to overhear. "Don't want no part in this." He pulled a coin from his pocket and held it up so it caught the moon. From the dull reflection Slocum thought he spied a double eagle. Real? Fake? No way of telling.

The man climbed up on the corral fence and sat so he had his profile to Slocum. This was definitely the whip-wielding Rafe.

"They're payin' me damn good money, but what am I doin'? I can get myself kilt. Kilt dead! Or the marshal might throw me in jail."

Slocum worked closer, wondering if he gained any leverage over Bulwer by kidnapping his teamster.

"Didn't know I had a prisoner in the back of my wagon. I didn't!"

Slocum sank to the ground, fading into the terrain as Rafe looked toward a barn.

"Can't do a thing about her. Can't. They'd kill me." Rafe muttered too low for Slocum to hear, then said, "Don't know she didn't want to come. Never said a word. She might be Bulwer's girlfriend. Real classy lady, like him with all them airs."

As Rafe continued to convince himself what he had done was all fine and legal, Slocum slipped around the corral and went to the barn so he could peer into a window. The glass had been smashed a long time ago, but this was a boon. Reflection from the rising moon wouldn't obscure what was inside. He chanced a quick look, then took a longer one around and saw nothing.

He ducked down when a woman moaned and was immediately answered by a gruff, "You keep your mouth shut, or I'll stuff the gag back in."

"Go to hell!"

Elena was immediately stifled. Slocum pictured Bulwer's gunman cramming a rag into her mouth to keep her quiet. He didn't take time to wonder what else they might have done to her. The only reason to bring her to the hideout was . . .

He froze when two men approached from the direction of the forge.

"Dan's had plenty of time with her. 'Bout time for us to show her what real men can do."

His partner laughed as they entered the barn. Slocum drew his six-shooter and then slid it back into the holster. Gunplay would only get both him and Elena killed.

"Boss wants you to do some of the fine milling on a new batch of lead."

"Don't he ever rest?" the one who'd been identified as Dan groused. "The way he works, you'd think there was a deadline."

"There is for the Pueblo job. Big gold shipment moving down on the train from Denver, end of next week."

"It was supposed to be in two!" Dan protested.

"Something in Denver spooked the banker, so he changed the schedule. Don't matter none. We'll have plenty of the lead slugs ready to go."

"Yeah, we'll have to work around the clock, though."

"Get on over there," the other newcomer said. "How was she?"

"Dee-light-ful," Dan said, laughing. "She's a real frisky one, too. Be careful. She bites."

"That why you got her gagged?"

"Naw, she screams."

"But I like that."

All three men laughed, causing a cold anger to settle in Slocum's gut.

Dan left, hurrying toward the forge. Slocum took a step toward him, then stopped. There wasn't any way he could get revenge for what the counterfeiter had done to Elena. The best way to help the woman was to keep it from happening again. Twice more.

He stepped back, looked at the barn, and saw how rickety it was. Bulwer had found an abandoned farm and taken it over, not bothering to repair anything but the corral before setting up his forge and rolling mill. Circling the barn, Slocum found a spot at the rear where varmints had gnawed through the wood and left a sizable hole. He looped his fingers around the boards and pulled slowly, trying not to make too much noise. When the nails tore free with a loud squeak, he was sure the men would come to investigate.

The coldness moved from Slocum's gut to his heart when he poked his head through and saw that they weren't paying attention to anything but Elena. They had her wrists bound and had dangled her from an overhead beam. Her toes barely raked the dirty floor. She was naked to the waist. Moonlight angled in from a hole in the roof, turning her breasts into silvery mounds.

One man walked close to her and kissed her bare breast. She flinched away and started to swing. She would have moaned louder except they had left the gag in her mouth.

"Lemme try that." The other man stepped up and tried to suckle at her tit. The more Elena struggled, the worse it became for her. Slocum knew the pressure on her shoulders but couldn't guess at the emotional torture she endured.

Again he touched his pistol and again he knew this wasn't the way to stop her rape. A shot would bring the rest of the gang down on his head in a flash.

Slocum squeezed through the hole he'd made in the wall and rolled to crouch behind a stall wall. He peered around the edge of the stall to get a better idea how to prevent the men from torturing Elena.

One now held her legs while the other fumbled at her skirt. In seconds she would be completely naked and hung up like a side of beef. The more she struggled, the more the pair liked it. They laughed and made lewd comments. One ran his hand up under her skirt. From the way she reacted, Slocum knew where the man had thrust his fingers. Elena arched her back and tried to flip over, to get away from the sexual punishment.

"You like that, don't you? Jist wait till I get the real thing shoved up there. I—"

He never said another word. Slocum drew his Colt, stepped out, and swung it as hard as he could, the butt crushing into the back of the man's skull. He dropped to his knees, clutching his head. Slocum cursed himself for not being stronger, but the ride had drained him of energy. Even the long sleep had failed to rejuvenate him.

Then he found himself caught up in a bear hug, his arms pinned at his sides by the other man's powerful embrace.

Slocum grunted. The man lifted him off his feet and began bending him backward. Slocum fought. To give in meant having his spine snapped. He tried to get off a shot. Even if he hit the outlaw in the leg, it would break the grip.

The world started to collapse into a single bright spot, blackness all around. Slocum let out a scream to coordinate his strength, to startle the man dealing out such punishment to him—anything to win free. It didn't work.

"I don't know who you are, but you're gonna be real dead mighty quick." The outlaw grunted, and redoubled his effort to break Slocum in half.

Then something smashed into Slocum's face, knocking him to one side. Long, trim, white legs came out of nowhere and encircled the outlaw's head.

"Elena," Slocum gasped out, dropping to his knees. She had swung up and locked her legs around the man's head. With a convulsive jerk, she spun about, still dangling from her bound wrists. The loud crack as the man's neck broke filled the barn, and then there was only silence. Even then she did not release her hold. She swung back and forth until Slocum thought she would tear the man's head from his shoulders.

"Enough," he said, standing up painfully. "He's dead."

He thought she said through her gag, "Not dead enough," but he couldn't tell. His arms circled her legs as he lifted enough for her to free her ropes from the hook above. When he had to support her weight, he wasn't up to it and collapsed. She landed on top of him.

"Sorry," Slocum said. "I'm a mite tuckered out."

She pushed away and disappeared from his field of vision. He sucked in huge drafts of air, the pain in his ribs going away but the one in his side remaining. No matter how much punishment the outlaws delivered to him, it was always Elena's stab wound that caused him the most grief.

He sat up and found himself peering into the bore of a .44.

The outlaw he had clubbed propped himself against a stall. Blood flowed freely down the side of the man's head and turned his collar and shoulder into a red swamp. Slocum was sorry he hadn't delivered a second blow and finished him off. If he hadn't been so weak, he would have.

"I don't know who the hell you are, but I want you to know it's Billy Bee who's gonna kill you." Billy Bee let out a loud howl, and Slocum thought he was a goner. Then the outlaw fell facedown onto the floor. A pitchfork stuck up out of his back.

A naked, panting Elena stared at the second man she had killed in the span of a couple minutes.

"Is he dead?"

"Yeah," Slocum said.

"Damn, I wanted to kill him some more." She kicked the corpse with her bare foot, fell to her knees, and pounded at the man's back with her bound hands. Slocum let her drain some of the anger, then took her in his arms and held her. To his surprise, she didn't cry. She shook all over but that could as easily have been from being naked in the cold spring night as emotional reaction.

"Let me get you free." Slocum fumbled with the ropes but finally got them off her wrists. Her hands were covered in her own blood from where the ropes had cut into her flesh. He had to help her dress.

"I want to kill them all. Especially Anton Bulwer. He told them they could have me. Just like I was a cheap whore. Worse, he *paid* them to do this to me. He *paid* them!"

Slocum rolled over the one with the pitchfork in his spine and found a couple coins. Bogus? Real? He didn't bother to check. He tucked them away in his pocket, then found another pair in the pocket of the man Elena had almost decapitated.

"We've got to get out of here," Slocum said, taking her arm. She yanked free.

"Not until every last one is dead!"

"We need the law to handle this. The marshal. A federal marshal."

"I'm a detective, dammit. A Pinkerton! They can't get away with doing this to me!"

He held her close again. This time she did cry. He felt her hot tears soaking into his shirt, mingling with the blood already there. Carefully, he steered her toward the rear of the barn. When Bulwer found his two henchmen dead, there'd be hell to pay. The best he could hope for was to get a decent head start—and find a place to make a stand.

After she dressed hurriedly in her torn clothing, Slocum and Elena slid out into the chilly night air and began their escape.

18

"My horse, where's my horse?"

Slocum put his arm around Elena to keep her moving away from the corral, where Rafe still sat on an upper rail. He no longer talked to himself and might have been asleep. Slocum didn't want to take the chance of being seen. If the teamster let out a cry, the rest of the counterfeiters might have flocked over to see what was wrong. It wouldn't take long for them to find the dead pair in the barn and then all hell would be out for lunch.

"We'll ride double. My horse can take the extra weight. You don't weigh that much."

"You've lost some weight, too," Elena said. She tried to turn and go back, but Slocum herded her into the dark until she finally stumbled along. As she started to speak, he whispered a warning in her ear.

"Yes, yes, the sons of bitches. Mustn't find us. But how will I get my revenge?"

"Let Marshal Atkinson do it. Let the law lock them up forever." He knew counterfeiting was about the only crime that Bulwer and his henchmen were likely to be convicted of, but he had to soothe Elena to get her away. Retribution could come later. He remembered how she had stabbed the man in the back with the pitchfork.

And the sight of the man with his neck broken as surely as if a hangman's noose had been dropped around it would linger for years.

"There's my horse."

"We can't ride back up the trail. I was trying to get away. Back of the wagon. Looked out," she said, her thoughts still disjointed. "But it was steep. They'll see us if they follow."

"There has to be another way back to Leadville. We'll ride north in the canyon until we find another trail up to the main road." His mind raced. That might take days to find, but he wasn't in any hurry. And for Elena, time meant nothing. She was still in shock from what had happened to her.

He stepped up into the saddle and felt all the strength flow from him like a dam had broken. He reached down and almost tumbled from the saddle as he pulled her up behind him. The horse dutifully set out. Slocum wanted to gallop, but carrying twice the weight, the mare would falter and might break a leg in the darkness. The thin slice of moon gave the landscape an eerie quality. Slocum jumped at shadows and more than once had his six-shooter halfway out of the holster as a coyote or fox poked a head out of vegetation to see the intruders.

By sunup he was about ready to fall out of the saddle. Elena rode behind him, arms locked around his waist. After rubbing his eyes, he saw a spot where they could hole up for a few hours. He needed the rest or they'd never get all the way back to Leadville.

"We can rest," he said. "There, in the trees out of sight."

"Have you been hiding our trail?"

"No need," he said, looking up. The heavy clouds that had moved in just after sunrise might have given Leadville its name. A fat drop of rain spatted against the brim of his hat. "The rain will wash away our tracks."

"They'll come for us."

"I know."

He rode into the trees just as the rain began pelting down more heavily. He was thinking how to use his slicker to cover them both when he saw a ramshackle shed. Luck finally smiled on him. Like so much else in this part of Colorado, the cabin, if he wanted to grace it with such a noble name, had been abandoned a long time back as richer strikes had sent the miners racing to find new fortunes. He slid off the saddle and caught Elena as she clumsily dismounted.

"What about your horse?"

"There's room inside." He led the horse to the door, but the mare refused to enter. He let Elena precede him, then took off the tack and led the horse around back. Again luck favored him. The lean-to attached to the rear of the cabin was in better shape than the building itself. Making sure the horse was secure, Slocum stumbled back around and into the cabin. Elena had spread out the blanket in a corner of the room higher than the rest, in case the roof leaked.

As Slocum went to where she was already curled up in a tight ball, he heard the tap-tap of rain on the brim of his hat. He looked up and saw a dozen leaks, but they were still drier inside than out. He pulled his slicker from his saddlebags and draped it over them.

As he lay down, she uncurled and then fit against him like spoons in a drawer. He would have enjoyed it, but he was so dog tired he slipped off to sleep in seconds.

Slocum wasn't sure how much later that he felt fingers working on his gun belt and pulling it away. He reached down and caught a slender wrist.

"What are you doing?" he asked.

"I want to forget, John. I want you to make me forget."

"Are you sure, after they raped you?"

"You can make me forget it all, if only for a few minutes. Please."

He rolled over. As he did so, he looked up, surprised to see blue sky through the roof. He felt as if he had slept for a hundred years, yet it was daylight.

"We slept the day around," she said.

"No, this is the morning after we escaped."

"No," Elena said firmly. "I was awake most of the past twenty-four hours. You slept so hard I worried you might have died."

Her hand slipped down under the waistband of his jeans and found a sleeping giant. His manhood stirred as she stroked along it.

"But you can't be dead. *This* isn't dead."

Slocum rolled the rest of the way and faced her. Tears streaked the dirt on her cheeks. He gently kissed her closed eyes, then worked down to her perfect lips. The propriety of making love to her so soon after she had been raped and tortured bothered him, but she wanted it. Her insistent squeezing on him showed that. He continued drawing his lips over hers, lower, across her slender throat, back to an ear. Somehow they rubbed against each other and buttons were opened and clothing discarded. It might have taken an hour or a few minutes. Slocum hardly knew or cared.

His hands roamed over the curves and depressions of her valley, eliciting moans of pleasure that grew in intensity. When she gasped as his finger invaded her and stroked over that tender territory, he was achingly hard and needy. Rolling over, he fitted himself between her legs. She opened for him.

He hesitated.

"Yes, John, do it. I need you to wipe out the bad memories."

His hips moved slightly, touching her nether lips, now slick with her inner juices. Another movement inserted the plum tip of his manhood and then he was unable to move any slower. He slipped all the way into her. Elena let out a cry of pleasure, arched her back, and began grinding her hips down to take him even deeper into her heated center.

For a moment, Slocum and Elena hung there, in a limbo of warmth and tightness, hearts beating together, their needs merging. Then he began slipping back and forth, moving faster, with greater passion. The white heat mounted in him, and he soon exploded within her.

She clawed at his back and crammed herself harder against him, their crotches slamming hard. And then it was over. Slocum slipped down atop her, then rolled over to hold her close. She pressed herself into him. He felt tears again but said nothing, did nothing. Eventually the tears stopped and Elena spoke.

"We have to get back to Leadville to stop them."

"Are you going to get them arrested or kill them?"

"Whatever it takes to stop them," she said. She looked up, her eyes brimming with unshed tears. "I won't lie. I want them all dead, but seeing them sent off to a federal prison forever and ever will be good enough. Why does it bother you that I want to kill Bulwer for what he's done?"

"It changes you," Slocum said. "I don't want you changed."

"Like killing men has changed you?"

Slocum paused, then said, "Yes."

Nothing more passed between them for long minutes, then they rose, wordlessly began dressing, and gathered the tack to saddle his mare. Only when they were well on their way up the valley and had found another road curling up the side to the road running along the ridge to Leadville did Elena say anything more.

"I sent Mr. Pullman a telegram before I was kidnapped. He knows everything we did up to that point."

"I reckoned you'd do something like that. You don't think he'll do anything stupid?" Slocum had to ask, but he knew the answer, no matter what Elena said. If there was anything Josiah Pullman could do to scare off the counterfeiters, he'd do it and never realize what he had done.

In spite of his dour thoughts, Slocum had to laugh.

"What's so funny, John?"

"Just remembering how Pullman looked with the phony mustache glued on his upper lip."

"It was funny, wasn't it?" Elena chuckled, and Slocum counted that as success. For the moment. She would probably never forget what Bulwer's henchmen had done to her, but whatever took the sharp edges off that burr was worthwhile.

"What do we do?" Slocum asked.

"The only place to begin is with the freighter."

"Rafe," Slocum supplied. "He's not too keen on his part, but I don't think he understands what he's doing for Bulwer."

"It doesn't matter. He's breaking the law."

"He might be a useful wedge to drive between Bulwer and the rest of his gang." They tossed back and forth possible ways of bringing the counterfeiter to justice, but Slocum worried more that Rafe had been sent south with a load of fake coins. He had overheard the gang talking about a robbery in Pueblo. To catch Bulwer, it might be necessary to ride south.

"There's Leadville," Elena said with a catch in her voice.

"Nobody'll know," he told her. "You don't have a sign tacked to your back. If you don't mention it, nobody'll know."

"If I report to the marshal . . ."

"I'd advise against it. Atkinson might be honorable enough about not spreading it around town how you were used, but his deputies don't have enough brains between them to outthink a mule. For them, it'd be a story to get free drinks at the nearest saloon."

"The counterfeiting is the crime that matters," she said, a catch in her voice.

"That's the one that'll put them behind bars."

They rode in silence the rest of the way to the hotel.

Elena dropped from the horse and hurried inside, not bothering to look back. He hoped she would stay in her room the rest of the day while he prowled about town hunting for Rafe or any of the counterfeiters who might have come back.

For the life of him, he couldn't imagine why Bulwer would let any of his gang come to Leadville. A misspoken word, a drunken boast, a gunfight—all could ruin Bulwer's plans for making himself a millionaire by passing fake gold coins.

Slocum rode directly to Rafe's freight company and dropped to the ground in front of the office. He made sure his six-shooter was loaded and ready before he went inside. The metallic click of a shotgun hammer drawing back stopped him dead in his tracks.

"I might have known you would show up eventually, Slocum," said Marshal Atkinson.

"What brings you here, Marshal?"

"Now, now, Slocum, don't play coy with me. I got witnesses that saw you come into this office a couple days back. Shots were fired. A gent I haven't identified yet was left out back by the corral with three holes in his gut. And Rafe? The owner? Can't seem to find hide nor hair of him. Might be you can help with some of this?"

"Either pull the trigger or lower that scattergun," Slocum said in a tone that warned the marshal he had crossed the line. The marshal swung the shotgun around so Slocum wasn't in the direct line of fire. All it would take was a quick move to bring it back to center on its target since the lawman kept his finger curled around the trigger.

"Well, Slocum? I don't have all day to wait for an answer."

"You been here for the last couple days? Sounds as if all you've got is time."

"You kill a man out back?"

"Any shots fired from the man's gun?"

"Was," Atkinson allowed. "So?"

"Whatever happened must have been self-defense. You see the owner of this business? I've got some freight I want shipped."

"That's another part of the mystery. Rafe Johnson's disappeared, him and his wagon."

"That sounds like he's out working."

"Asked around town. Nobody here's hired him."

"Times are hard for a teamster in Leadville. All the short hauling's done by teams owned by the mines. Rafe might have driven elsewhere to look for work to keep body and soul together."

"But you wouldn't know anything about that, now would you, Slocum?"

"Apparently not if I came here looking for him. If I want to ship . . . what I'm shipping."

"What might that be, Slocum?" The marshal looked at him hard but Slocum didn't waver.

"I'll let you know. If there's nothing else, Marshal, I find myself in powerful need of a drink."

Atkinson waved him from the office. As he stepped into the street, Slocum considered what the marshal had told him—and what he hadn't. Rafe's disappearance was of interest but only because a body had been found at his corral. Atkinson didn't seem to know that Bulwer or any members of his gang were involved.

That suited Slocum. He wanted the reward offered by the Pinkertons.

A commotion from a nearby saloon drew him. He poked his head through the doorway and looked around, spotting a man in a plaid suit making a fuss at the far end of the long bar. He went to the barkeep and asked, "What's the row?"

"He just got in from Denver, he says, and he doesn't have money to pay for his drink."

"I'll pay for it," Slocum said, fingering in his pocket one of the coins he'd taken from any number of the dead members of Bulwer's gang.

"He's a deadbeat. You don't hafta give him no charity."

"Give him this to pay for his drink." Slocum pulled out a coin, balanced it in his hand, and figured it was a counterfeit. The weight was about right—about. He hoped it was a fake. He didn't want to pay for Josiah Pullman's drink with a real coin. Slocum dropped it on the bar and listened hard. A smile came to his lips. Bogus. He shoved it across to the bartender.

"Your money."

Slocum started to leave. The barkeep called out, "You ain't bought yerse'f a drink!"

"Later," Slocum said. He wanted Pullman to raise a fuss about a counterfeit coin to see how big a hornet's nest the Pinkerton detective could stir up.

19

Slocum crept back to the hotel and went up the back stairs. He hesitated at the door to Elena's room, then turned the knob with one smooth, quiet motion and went in. She lay on the bed, still dressed and sleeping deeply. He considered leaving, but other than the stable, there wasn't anywhere he would rather stay. Annoying Jethro, the room clerk, would only create a stir he didn't want.

If things went well, there'd be plenty of disturbance in Leadville by the morning.

He pulled up a chair, positioned it by the bed, then put his feet up on the edge of the mattress and leaned back. Within seconds, he, too, was asleep.

He came awake when he heard shouts down in the lobby. Slocum checked to be sure that Elena was still sleeping, then left the room, hand on his six-shooter as he went down the stairs.

"I want him arrested!" Josiah Pullman shouted. "I am an agent of the Pinkerton Detective Agency, and I hereby proclaim him a counterfeiter!"

"You take care of him," the man Pullman accused said to

the clerk. "He's so stinkin' drunk there's no reasonin' with him."

"Leave and I will shoot you!" Pullman drew his gun with a flourish and waved it about. Slocum pulled his, ready to shoot if the man he had accosted went for the six-shooter at his hip.

"What kind of flophouse do you run here?" the man demanded of Jethro. "I work for the Jolly Ollie Mine Company. I'm a geologist and will not be treated this way."

"Look, mister, put down yer damn smoke wagon," Jethro said. "You got no call wavin' it 'round like that."

Slocum crouched at the head of the stairs so he could watch this drama play itself out. The geologist turned so Slocum got a better look at him. At one time or another, Slocum was sure he had seen all of Bulwer's gang. Unless this was a new one, perhaps working for Timmins or another in Denver or some other city, the accosted man was exactly as he claimed.

"I demand that you fetch the marshal in this godforsaken town. I demand justice." Pullman still waved his six-shooter about like he was leading a Fourth of July parade.

"I can agree to that," the geologist said. "And by damn, I'll get my justice. You'll rot in jail for a month if I have my way."

"And you will go to prison for a hundred years. Passing counterfeit coins! You are one of the infamous Anton Bulwer gang, and I have brought you to justice."

Slocum almost went down to interrupt when Atkinson and his deputy Clem came in, Jethro trailing behind and yammering.

"Shut up, Jethro," the marshal said. He sized up the situation and said, "I'll have this gent clapped into jail right away . . . Mr. Dunbar."

"Thank heavens, Atkinson. I thought everyone in this town had gone stark raving mad!"

"You're in league! You and the sheriff!"

"I'm the marshal," Atkinson said, turning. He nodded. Clem swung his pistol expertly and clipped Pullman a couple inches above the right ear. He dropped like he had been poleaxed. Clem grunted as he caught Pullman under the arms and began dragging him out of the lobby.

"You haven't been to town in a month of Sundays, Mr. Dunbar. This mean Ollie's hit a new vein?"

"That remains to be seen, but Mr. Olafson is a shrewd judge of mineral. He only summons me to verify the claim when he thinks he can afford my bill."

"Might make him another million," Atkinson said, nodding sagely. "I'll tend to this crazy coot, and you can buy me a drink after you get back from the mine."

"I've told you before, Marshal, I cannot divulge anything about what I find until Mr. Olafson authorizes it."

Slocum saw the geologist check to be sure Jethro heard his solemn declaration, then gave Atkinson a broad wink that the clerk couldn't see. The two men had a working arrangement of some standing, from the look of it. What Atkinson would do with the information—good or bad— from the potential strike was anyone's guess, but it undoubtedly benefited both men.

Atkinson and Dunbar left, and Jethro returned to his chair behind the desk. Slocum slipped out without anyone noticing him, stepped into the street, and headed for the jailhouse. Pullman had done as well as Slocum had hoped. If he had given him a script, the Pinkerton could not have played his part better, drawing attention to himself, to Bulwer's gang, and that he was here to stop the counterfeiters.

Slocum knew the deputy was taking Pullman directly to the lockup, so he stopped in the closest saloon. It was early in the morning, but a few miners were working on beers. He called out loudly for the barkeep.

"I'm celebrating," he announced for all to hear.

"Do tell. Mighty early for that, ain't it?" The bartender wiped a mug clean and dropped it in front of Slocum.

"Whiskey," Slocum said. "For everyone who wants it." He dropped one of the coins he had taken from Bulwer's gunman on the bar. From the way it rang, he knew it was phony. He didn't care. "I'm celebrating."

"How's that? You hit a big strike?" asked the nearest miner.

"You might say that. I'm going to bust the biggest counterfeiting ring in the West, and I'm getting a huge reward for it. He's going to tell Marshal Atkinson everything right now."

"Everything?" The barkeep looked skeptical.

"Everything. How the coins are made, where they get the material, and best of all, how they swap the fakes for real ones. They're making millions—but not any more thanks to that prisoner in the jail spilling his guts about the entire gang."

Slocum finished his drink, went to a saloon farther down the street, and repeated his claims. After the fourth saloon, he felt mighty fine and knew he had to stop drinking on an empty belly. Breakfast ought to be next, but Slocum wanted to clear his head and wait for the inevitable to happen. News spread fast when it was lubricated with enough liquor, and Slocum had greased well the rails gossip rolled on. He felt the town beginning to buzz around him with the news of a counterfeiter being caught and how he was spilling his guts to avoid the noose.

As he walked and listened, his tiny morsel of truth had blossomed into the most audacious story he had ever heard. A smile curled his lips. There was no way in hell Bulwer wouldn't hear about this and act.

If nothing else, he had to see which of his men had been caught. When he found out a Pinkerton detective was locked up, he might do any of a dozen things. Slocum was counting on him trying to kill Pullman and put an end to the rampant speculation about counterfeiting. Bulwer might shoot him through the jail window, have another of his men arrested and put in the same cell, where Pullman would mysteriously die, or even be so bold as to bail out the detective so he could kill him at his leisure after finding out what he really knew.

Or didn't know.

Josiah Pullman was nothing more than Slocum's stalking-horse in a scheme that was going to turn deadly.

Slocum found himself a spot catty-corner to the jailhouse. He settled down in a chair on the boardwalk, made sure his six-shooter rested easy and would come to hand fast, then tipped his hat down to shade his eyes, rocked back, and waited.

The wait turned into hours and his belly grumbled, but he didn't dare leave. He wished he had told Elena of his plan. She could have fetched him some food. When his mouth turned to cotton wool, he got up and drank from the rain barrel at the side of the building. Since it was mid-morning, the ice on the top had mostly melted, but the water left a cold trail all the way down into his gut. He splashed some water on his face and snapped alert.

A man he recognized as one of Bulwer's gang sauntered toward the jail. The counterfeiter looked around, trying to act nonchalant but failing. He was too focused on the jailhouse for that. When he vanished around back, Slocum considered following. The gunman might shoot Pullman and be on his way. Then Slocum sat down in the chair to see what would happen. If Bulwer's henchman intended to kill Pullman in an ambush, he would have brought his horse along for a quick getaway.

The man came back into view on the far side of the building, looked both ways along the street, then took off his black, floppy-brimmed hat and waved. Dust hung in the noontime air, sparkling motes darting about, but when the man kept waving, Slocum stood, drew his six-gun, and waited, the cocked weapon held at his side.

Two more of the gang rode up, leading a pair of horses.

Slocum grinned. He knew what they intended now. They weren't going to shoot Pullman where he sat in the cell. They wanted to kidnap him and find out what he knew. This made life easier for him. Slocum started walking toward the jail, six-shooter still at his side, as one rider joined the other outlaw on the ground, leaving one with the horses.

As the pair went into the jail, Slocum drew even with the man still in the saddle.

"Got a match?" Slocum asked.

"Go to hell—" That was as far as the outlaw got. Slocum reached up, grabbed a handful of duster, and yanked hard, unseating him. The man crashed to the ground and then lay still after Slocum applied the barrel of his six-gun alongside his head.

The horses reared and tried to run. Slocum took the reins and tucked them in an iron ring mounted at the side of the jailhouse. From inside he heard a commotion but no shots. Within seconds, the two outlaws boiled out, Josiah Pullman between them.

"Grab sky," Slocum shouted. One outlaw turned and lifted his six-shooter. He died with two of Slocum's slugs in his chest. The other tried to use Pullman as a shield. Slocum didn't much care if he shot the detective. "Surrender and you might live to see another sunrise."

"You're not takin' me. The boss'd kill me if—"

"Anton Bulwer?" Slocum asked. "I know him."

The surprise on the outlaw's face showed his momentary confusion. Slocum aimed and fired. Pullman yelped like a scalded dog and jerked free. The bullet had cut through his earlobe on its way past the counterfeiter's head.

"I got the drop on you, you slippery snake!" Atkinson came from the jail with a shotgun in his hand.

"Don't shoot!" Pullman cried from the ground. "I'm bleeding!"

The marshal, Slocum, and the outlaw fired at the same time. Slocum might have gotten in a killing shot, but there was no way to tell. At this range, the shotgun almost blew the counterfeiter into two hunks, neither alive.

"Don't, Slocum," Atkinson said, swinging the shotgun around.

"I'm on your side. I saved Pullman from getting spirited away by them."

"Do tell," Atkinson said dryly. "Now what is it you're angling for, Slocum?"

"The reward. They're part of the Bulwer gang."

"Can't rightly ask any questions of dead men and expect an answer."

"That one's still alive," Slocum said. The third outlaw moaned and weakly clawed at the ground. "He'll fess up to about everything."

"They're counterfeiters!" Pullman pulled himself upright and pointed. "They're part of Bulwer's gang. The one I told you about but you wouldn't listen and threw me into that terrible cell and—"

"Shut up, Pullman," the marshal said. He grabbed a handful of collar and pulled the outlaw Slocum had slugged to his feet. "Now you and me, we got some discussing to do." He shoved the dazed man inside, leaving Slocum with Pullman and two bodies already drawing flies and a crowd of curious townspeople.

"You fouled up everything, Slocum. You got me arrested and you killed those men and—"

"And you ought to wire your home office for the reward owed me. By the time the marshal finishes with his prisoner, he's going to know everything about Bulwer and his doings. If I hadn't come along, you'd be Bulwer's prisoner, and the marshal wouldn't be any the wiser where you were."

"I—"

"And I doubt if he'd much care, other than how it'd prick his pride losing a prisoner in a jailbreak. Chances would have been good he'd have told himself that you were out of his jurisdiction and forgotten the whole matter."

"He'd've let me stay their prisoner?" Pullman blanched.

Slocum turned when he saw Elena Warburton running up. He expected her to come to him but wasn't all that surprised when she dropped to her knees beside Pullman and began fussing over him.

He slid his six-shooter back into his holster and went inside to hear how Atkinson got the confession out of his new prisoner. There was a bit more to do but not that much more until Slocum could get the hell out of Leadville.

20

"Think you have a big enough posse, Marshal?" Slocum looked at the dozen men shifting nervously in their saddles, not a one of whom could be trusted not to bolt and run if shooting started. If they were this nervous before they reached the counterfeiters' hideout, Slocum guessed they would be worthless in a real fight.

Since Bulwer had a hint that his plans were coming apart, he would fight like a trapped rat—if he hadn't already hightailed it. At least Atkinson had been clever enough to lead his posse into the broad valley using a trail several miles even farther north of the one Slocum and Elena had taken to get back to Leadville. If even one of the deputies had tried approaching using the road Rafe had driven, Bulwer would have had an hour's notice of their approach.

"You think he is more cautious now than when he kidnapped me, John?"

Slocum looked at Elena, but she kept her eyes straight ahead. He understood. She had been through terrible torture, and he was part of it. He had rescued her and done what she'd asked to ease her pain, but now his mere pres-

181

ence reminded her of all that had happened at Bulwer's orders.

"He sent three men to fetch Pullman because he thought someone knew what he was up to. Since they haven't returned with Pullman yet, he's got to be edgy."

"I can pretend to be a prisoner. That means four of us could ride up to his front door and . . . knock." Pullman laughed at his own joke.

"That's a good way to get killed," Slocum said. "He's watching. Count on it. He's dangerous, and if anything looks wrong, he'll shoot first and never bother with questions."

"You are so inexperienced in the ways of the Pinkerton detective," Pullman said, chin lifted in the air, as if sniffing out wrongdoers. "Such deception is the heart of the Pinkerton method."

"Not many of you left in the field, then," Slocum said.

"That was uncalled for. Mr. Pullman is resourceful and clever," said Elena.

"You ready to ride, Slocum, or you going to set around all day and jaw?" Marshal Atkinson trotted up and looked at him, then the two detectives. "You want to hang back and protect them? Might be a good idea."

"I'll ride with you, Marshal." Slocum and the lawman took off, leaving Elena and Pullman behind, muttering about civilians and ways of detection.

"Tell me everything about this hideout, Slocum," Atkinson said. "I remember it belonged to a Mormon family what tried farming here. Never sure what happened to them but got reports the farm had been abandoned nigh on a year back."

"You ever look for them?"

"Out of my jurisdiction."

"Still is," Slocum said.

"I'm making an exception for this Anton Bulwer fellow. He tried to make a fool out of me busting a prisoner from my jail. That bruises my reputation and makes me eager to prevent him from doing whatever it is that he's doing."

Slocum had to laugh. He had told the marshal what went on here. So had Pullman and so had Elena, when Pullman let her get a word in edgewise.

"I can't go accusing a man of counterfeiting until I see some proof," Atkinson said with mock indignation. "Of course, those papers about him working for the U.S. Treasury, how he got himself fired, and the other documents the Pinkertons gave me strongly suggest Bulwer is one mean gent."

"We're getting close," Slocum said. He pointed to the curl of smoke drifting lazily into the clear sky. A bit of rain would have helped them sneak closer by shrouding their approach, but the day had bloomed bright and fresh as a daisy.

"You say Rafe was still in the camp when you got away with the little lady?"

"Are you worried for him?"

"It's like this. He's my wife's cousin and never got the hang of making a decent living. Being a teamster's as close as he's ever got to supporting himself. He's not a bad man."

"Sounded to me as if he didn't know what he was hauling," Slocum said.

"Good."

Atkinson motioned to six of the posse to circle wide and cut off retreat southward. Slocum knew they would never get into position before Bulwer spotted them—and so did Atkinson. Barely had the six galloped off when the lawman ordered the attack to begin.

Rifles and shotguns were the weapons of choice as they wheeled toward the buildings and tapped spurs against their horses' flanks.

Slocum levered a round into his Winchester just as the first slug ripped past him. They hadn't gotten twenty yards in their attack before Bulwer's sentry spotted them. Slocum fired as he rode, not finding any target but wanting to make the outlaws duck so they wouldn't fire into the posse. Whether this worked or Bulwer's men were already running for their lives, Slocum couldn't tell.

The posse swept through the camp, the fighting fierce and mercifully brief.

"Round them gents up and get them over here so I can look at them," Atkinson said.

Slocum had already noticed what the marshal was struggling to understand. Anton Bulwer was not among the handful of men captured.

"Where're the rest?" Atkinson demanded. He punctuated his question with a shotgun blast that tore off one man's toes. After a few minutes of interrogation, the marshal said to Slocum, "Looks like we rounded up the lot of them."

"You don't believe them that Bulwer is with Rafe on a wagon headed toward Pueblo, do you?"

"No reason not to," Atkinson said. "I didn't lose a man, and I'm keeping it that way."

"Marshal, we have them. We found the dies!" Pullman held up a thick cylinder and then turned the end so the lawman could see.

"That's what Bulwer used to imprint the lead slugs," Atkinson said. "Clem over there's found a whole lot of thin sheet gold. Make the milled lead slug, use the die to stamp out the pattern, then coat it with gold. That's the process, isn't it, Miss Warburton?"

"It is, Marshal," she said. She still refused to look in Slocum's direction. "From what we can tell of the supplies, there are very few fake coins in camp. We believe he is shipping them to Pueblo for another train robbery to substitute the coins."

"Every lawman I know would think it failed if there were these fakes still in the train car," Atkinson said, holding a counterfeit coin up to peer at it. "Bulwer could ride off with the real coins and do this again somewhere else, nobody knowing a crime had been committed. Clever devil. I'll be glad when my boys bring him in."

"The six that were supposed to cut off escape are going after him?" Slocum asked.

"If Rafe's driving, he won't have got far."

Slocum wondered if the freighter might not have a three- or four-day head start on the posse but said nothing. He looked around as Atkinson ordered the counterfeiters put on their horses, hands tied, and then led toward the trail winding up from the valley to go back to Leadville.

"Your reward will be waiting for you, Mr. Slocum," Elena said stiffly. "Your assistance has been quite instrumental in bringing these . . . these counterfeiters to justice." Her voice cracked but didn't break with emotion.

"It will be a sizable reward, too," Pullman said. "I am sure the Pinkerton Detective Agency will gift you with as much as one hundred dollars. Good work, man, leading us to these foul fiends so we could properly arrest them."

Elena started to speak, then clamped her mouth shut and lowered her eyes.

"Give my reward to Miss Warburton," Slocum said. "She's done more to earn it than I have."

"Why, she is an employee. I am not sure she—" Pullman swallowed hard when he saw Slocum's cold gaze. "Very well, I will do that very thing."

"Put in a recommendation on her, too. A commendation for outstanding work in the field."

"Why, uh, yes, that goes without saying. Come along, Miss Warburton. We want to tie up all the loose ends by aiding Marshal Atkinson with his interrogation of the prisoners."

Elena looked up at Slocum, started to speak, but then turned and ran off. He wondered if tears were streaming down her cheeks. He thought so.

The posse started back to Leadville with their prisoners. Pullman and Elena had possession of the dies used to make the fake coins. The counterfeiting ring had been broken.

In ten minutes, Slocum stood in the camp all alone. He looked into the mist-hazy south, then over at the barn where Elena had been tortured. Anton Bulwer might be with Rafe heading for Pueblo with the fake coins.

Slocum thought the counterfeiter was somewhere else. Near.

He listened hard but heard only the soft soughing wind blowing down the valley. Slocum checked his Colt before walking to the barn. Behind it he saw a tethered, saddled horse. He looked in the saddlebags and saw enough gold double eagles to let a man live in style, even at the Union Club in San Francisco, for quite a spell.

Softly approaching the side door into the barn, he chanced a quick peek around the corner. Nothing moved inside. He stepped in just as a bit of dirt and splintery wood fell from above. Reacting instantly, Slocum dropped into a gunfighter's crouch, pointed his six-shooter up, and fired the instant before Bulwer cut loose with a shotgun.

Slocum staggered back, fire burning his thighs. He recovered, stepped forward, and fired twice more, just to be sure. His first shot had ended the counterfeiter's life, but the additional rounds tearing through Bulwer's body made him feel better. The counterfeiter hung draped over the same beam that his henchmen had used to suspend Elena.

"So why were you in here?" Slocum asked softly. His only answer was whistling wind through the cracks in the side of the barn. Poking around got him nowhere. He found a lantern and after considerable effort got the wick trimmed and lit. Holding it high, he prowled throughout the barn until he came to a stall where the straw had been disturbed recently.

He kicked it away and saw a freshly dug hole, now filled in. The dirt hadn't been properly tamped down, but Bulwer might not have had the time. He had taken what he could from the camp and sacrificed his men so he could escape.

Anton Bulwer didn't strike Slocum as the kind of man who rode away empty-handed. The gold coins in his saddlebags were hardly enough for a man as clever as Anton Bulwer.

Before he began digging, Slocum had to bind his fresh wounds. Three buckshot pellets had ripped into his legs. Only the angle had saved him from serious injury. After tying bandages around his thighs and stanching the blood, only then did he start to dig. He didn't have to go down far before he hit a canvas sack.

He dragged it outside and into the afternoon sun. Gold coins spilled onto the ground in a glittering waterfall of wealth. Slocum caught his breath as he stared at the riches at his feet. He bent, picked one up, and bit down on it.

He laughed when his tooth sank into . . . real gold. Where Bulwer had gotten these coins hardly mattered. They were legal tender.

And they were John Slocum's reward for his part in stopping Anton Bulwer.

He recovered Bulwer's saddlebags and then filled his own with the coins from the barn, mounted, and headed north. Half the posse was riding south and he wanted to avoid them. Atkinson was taking the most direct trail with his prisoners back to Leadville.

Slocum rode north with a smile on his lips, a fortune in gold in his saddlebags, and only best wishes for Elena Warburton and her burgeoning career as a Pinkerton detective.

Watch for

SLOCUM'S REWARD

386th novel in the exciting SLOCUM series
from Jove

Coming in April!